Tour of Duty

Tour of Duty

By

William H. Coles

Second edition

No part of this book may be reproduced, stored in a retrieval system, or transmitted by any means without the written permission of the author.

Published 22 Nov, 2025
First edition published 1 Aug, 2022

Story in Literary Fiction www.storyinliteraryfiction.com

Cover and interior design by Susanne Howard

ISBN: 978-0-9601163-1-7

Dedication

For

Mary Elizabeth Hartnett

A unique, generous, and loving soul.

Tour of Duty

In the 1960s, the Cuban Missile Crisis and escalation of the Vietnam conflict, intensified the fears of the free world. The US military geared up for the worst. Thousands of young men were drafted into active military duty. Miles Ballard was a doctor in training and when drafted, chose the Berry Plan option for physicians, which would delay deployment until completion of a medical degree. Ballard finished his internship and was inducted to serve in the US Air Force in 1960.

PART ONE
1960–61

CHAPTER 1
Arrival

1960
France

Dense layers of gray clouds steeped with damp drifted to the east in the French sky over Paris. Miles Ballard lugged two brown leather suitcases and a backpack from baggage claim into the terminal at Orly International Airport. A woman in a flower-patterned, tea-colored dress cinched with a red, braided-cord belt at the waist, held up a cardboard packing-box lid with CAPTAIN BALLARD hand-printed in block letters. Miles approached her.

"Are you Captain Ballard?" she asked.

Miles nodded.

"Welcome," she said. "I'm Ingrid. From the base travel office."

He liked her look: about five feet, six inches, and waved, light-brown hair shimmered with a hint of gold. It touched her shoulders and accented the blue-green of her eyes, which fixated rather than roamed. Her thin lips formed a sincere, kind smile, if not attenuated. She seemed vulnerable in some way.

She moved to pick up one of his bags.

"I'll do that," he insisted. She looked athletic, but she was a woman, and he didn't feel right about her carrying his gear. "Where can I find the train to Châteauroux?"

"I have a military car and driver waiting," she said.

"You sure? I can take the train."

"It's my job! Grab your bags and get in the car!"

Something about her looks and personality made Miles feel better about his luck in missing his first French train ride that he had imagined with pleasure on his flight from LaGuardia.

As Ingrid led him to the exit, a disheveled man wearing coveralls and a plaid wool shirt, his coal-black hair streaked with gray, approached. "*Cochon!*" he snarled and spat near Miles's feet. Miles turned to face him.

"Come on," Ingrid said urgently.

"What does that word mean?"

"Ignore him."

"No, what does it mean?"

"It means pig."

"Derogatory?"

"Very. It's your uniform."

"I'm required to wear a uniform while traveling on duty and in public."

"I know that! But don't pick a fight on your arrival in France. Keep walking, and don't look back!"

They exited, and she led him toward a military gray-green sedan waiting at the curb, a uniformed airman driver behind the wheel.

"Why was he so angry?" Miles asked.

"Well, you remind him that it was American soldiers who died to win the war on Normandy beach. A lot of nationalities died, but he doesn't like the Americans' conceit about it. And he really doesn't like anyone not French."

"I just wanted to talk to him."

"That's not recommended. Just not right for the situation. Besides, don't pick fights with someone eight inches taller than you."

"But if you treat people with civility, they're less hostile," Miles said.

"That's naive. He really doesn't like you!"

"You don't like me either, do you?"

"Well, I haven't known you long enough." She smiled slightly.

"You think I'm arrogant?"

"All American military men are arrogant."

"So why are you working for them?"

"My husband's a doctor at the base. We can use the money."

She must know I'll be a doctor at the base. "I assume you married him for his potential wealth?" he smiled.

"Smartass." She jabbed his arm in jest with her closed fist. "I know you're a doctor, and I guarantee I wouldn't marry you for your salary or personality."

"That hurt," he said.

"Your callow feelings?"

"My vulnerable soul."

Exhausted, he slept on the two-and-a-half-hour drive to Châteauroux air base.

CHAPTER 2

Induction

1960
US Air Station, Châteauroux, France

On the first day after arrival, Miles signed documents, listened to tape-recorded instructions on military procedures, received a health examination, and was welcomed to the Air Force by the first personnel officer with a cup of coffee. At the end of the day, he received a note from the hospital adjutant, Emile Macron, to meet the hospital commander, Colonel Barney Springer, at 18:00 in the officer's club bar.

Springer arrived forty-five minutes late and offered no apology. He told Miles to sit next to him and held up an index finger to signal the bartender.

"Bring him Blanton's Single Barrel," Springer said. "My favorite," he noted to Miles and back to the bartender, "Make that a double straight up for me."

"I prefer water, no ice, please," Miles said to the bartender.

"Ridiculous," Springer snapped. "That's handmade Kentucky bourbon. Best of the best."

"I don't drink . . ."

"On the rocks for him," Springer insisted to the bartender.

"I prefer just water," Miles said, ignoring Springer's stern stare.

Springer looked from the bartender to Miles, "You don't start your tour of duty in France with water. Not on my watch," he said. "You a teetotaler?"

"I've been on and off call for years. An alcoholic drink never occurs to me, really. Eventually, I want to be a surgeon."

"Goddamn, boy. We gotta lighten you up a bit. A Sancerre Rouge, then," Springer said to the bartender, who stood waiting as if this happened often.

"I'll have a Coke, please," Miles said.

The bartender hesitated, standing ramrod straight, waiting for instructions from his superior. Springer shook his head. "That won't do," he said. "Just the wine for him," he said to the bartender.

The drinks were served with salted peanuts in an unadorned, pressed-glass dish on a paper napkin.

"When do I start seeing patients?" Miles asked.

"When you complete payroll in accounting," Springer replied. "Then get your quarters ready. You got your uniforms?"

"I've got one from basic training."

"Get more."

"Where do I get uniforms? "

"Sarge knows. They're issued for officers, and any tailored alterations are at your own expense. Check with Pringle about your clothing allowance."

"Are patients being scheduled?"

"They'll start scheduling new patients next week. Until you build a following, you get walk-ins, routine checkups, emergencies, and non-specific referrals. Pringle will put you on the call schedule."

"How often?"

"About once every two weeks."

A waiter approached. "Dinner, sir?" he asked Springer.

"Just the drinks," Springer replied.

As the waiter moved away, Springer confidentially leaned toward Miles. "It's all essentially free here. A few non-free charges get deducted from a doctor's pay before taxes," he grinned. "Commissioned officers got advantages."

Miles stayed quiet.

"And you've got triage evaluation on Wednesday," Springer said.

"What is that?"

"Takes three hours. They got people commandeered to play victims with made-up wounds lying around in the dirt. Victims of a plane crash. A few "dead" people. You make a diagnosis, direct to preserve life on the spot, and direct transfer to the nearest appropriate facility for treatment. You'll be graded. You don't pass, you retake until you do."

"Where do I learn?"

"It's triage. You know what triage is?"

That irritated Miles. "I know what triage is."

"Sir," said Springer.

"What?"

Springer frowned, It's . . . I know what triage is, *sir!*' You get it?"

"But what does triage expect of me?"

"Sir! Damn it."

"Sir."

"Sarge will tell you. There's a manual."

Aggravated, Springer stood abruptly and pointed to Miles's untouched glass of wine.

"Suck it up, Ballard. You got a lot to learn."

"Suck it up?" Miles asked.

"Say sir! Damn it. Drink it, man!"

Miles took a sip.

Springer pursed his lips as if Miles's reluctance debased him.

"Command is hung up on triage. They're scared shitless we'll all die in a nuclear attack," Springer grimaced, glancing over the restaurant crowd.

A nuclear attack–not a comforting thought, Miles thought. "Thank you–sir."

Springer waved a dismissal to the bartender. "Follow me," he said to Miles, "I'll introduce you to some cool dudes that can take care of anything you need. Then I gotta go."

***

Two days later, a military school bus shuttled Miles to the acre-and-a-half field test site. The fenced enclosure was draped with opaque canvas panels. Forty-plus people with simulated injuries lay scattered over foliage and scrubby grass.

An airman struck a brass gong to start the exercise. An observer and a medical assistant accompanied Miles into the enclosure.

The victims had realistic fake wounds created with collages of plaster, plastics, molded rubber, and red fluids. Some had "exposed bones," others had "chest wounds" that, when the victim pumped air through a tube from a bulb in the hand, suggested a punctured lung. The air hung heavy with sham moans and cries for help.

Miles evaluated mental state, the status of the airway, bleeding, and shock, and dictated lifesaving measures to a nurse. An assistant recorded vital signs and personal data. Throughout the exercise, Miles tagged each victim with a cloth rag around the right arm—red for immediate life-saving intervention required, yellow signaling treatment could be delayed up to four hours, green for the "walking" injured, white for no treatment required, and black for the deceased. Two and a half hours later, the gong sounded again, signaling an end to the exercise. All victims had been prioritized on the spot and/or scheduled for transfer.

Outside the triage area, Miles asked the observer how he did.

"Can't say, sir."

"You must know if I passed?"

"Colonel Springer evaluates the results for hospital staff."

"Isn't that a conflict of interest?"

"Why?"

"Springer's staff benefits from high scores."

"We're observers. I make no judgments."

"Is my evaluation based on quality of care?" Miles asked.

"No, sir," the observer said. "I record the accuracy of your diagnosis and the time it takes you to make decisions. That's what triage is, not care or outcome."

Later that afternoon, Colonel Springer called Miles into his office.

"Did I pass?" Miles asked.

Springer shrugged dismissively.

"Does that mean I passed?"

Springer nodded almost imperceptibly.

"Thank you, sir." Miles prepared to leave.

"And Ballard."

"Yes, sir."

"I've assigned you to the General as his personal physician."

"Really, sir. Am I qualified?"

"It's for you to travel with the General when he asks. You take care of him personally, too, and the family when they need you. They're all healthy. Anyone is qualified."

"Shouldn't the General choose his own doctor? I've never met him."

"I told you, say 'sir'!"

"Why me, sir?"

"Most docs don't like him, and you're available. So, you're his personal doc."

"I don't understand."

"Say, 'sir'! He wants a doctor. He isn't concerned with qualifications or who you are, for that matter. For chrissakes, it's prestige for him. And it's got nothing to do with health. Anybody alive, doctor or not, could do it. You're the new man at the bottom of the heap. You're his doctor! His General medical officer."

"Wouldn't he want a flight surgeon?"

"They're trained to keep people in the cockpit. Exams and checkups. It's you that does the grubby stuff."

"What about my practice?"

"The General will only need you three or four days a month. You finally get it? And say, sir!"

"Yes, sir. Thank you—uh, sir."

In the hallway, away from Springer's door, Emile, the adjutant, approached Miles with a tenuous smile. "How did triage go?"

"I passed."

"Did Springer tell you that you tied with three others for the second-highest score recorded in the last three years?" Emile smiled widely.

"No. He didn't seem impressed at all."

"Well, don't sweat it. That's Springer. It's his routine. He wants to debase you, make you worry a little."

"I don't get it."

"He doesn't like anyone smarter or better trained than he is."

"Damn. And I've got to be a General's physician too."

"The General has his hand in everyone's cookie jar, but he's not a bad guy. Even though he *is* a serious hypochondriac."

Miles shook his head. He couldn't imagine caring for a one-star general; they didn't seem like regular humans. "How can I get along with Springer, sir?" he asked.

"Just do the best you can. Everyone has problems."

"Thank you, sir."

"You can relax with me, Ballard. I'm a lieutenant. Most people call me Pepper."

"Thanks for being straight with me," Miles said. "I appreciate it."

CHAPTER 3

A Colleague

1960
Miles

Two days later, Miles started patient care; he sat behind a gray-painted metal desk in his exam room reading yesterday's *International Herald Tribune*. A small rectangular window let in a smidgen of morning light that combined with the fluorescent light from overhead to give the room a chalk-white glare. He had only one patient scheduled, for midmorning.

After a knock, a short, stocky doctor entered so quickly that Miles had no time to respond to the intrusion.

"Got a minute?" the doctor asked. He crossed over to the desk, shook Miles's hand, and, uninvited, pulled up a straight-backed metal chair to sit to the side of the desk, close to Miles. Curly black hair covered his ears and straggled down to his eyebrows. A brown stain streaked his Air Force–issue dark tie, whose knot sagged. His scuffed and scarred black shoes lacked any shine, and his dark-brown eyes and ephemeral smile betrayed both irreverence and irony.

Miles introduced himself. "Miles Ballard."

"Oliver Stern, here. Welcome to Europe in the Cold War."

He looks like a dissident, Miles thought. But he only said, "What's up?"

"I need a friend," Oliver replied.

Miles's interest was piqued by this disheveled doctor now; Miles smiled inwardly. "No problem. I haven't made a friend since I arrived. You've got no competition."

"I'm here to tell you this place drives me berserk," Oliver said. "And it's alarmingly friendless. You'll be insane in six months."

Miles smiled outwardly this time.

"You trained in Boston," Oliver continued. 'Top of the profession. You're sitting here waiting to heal your fellow man, and you've got almost nothing to do."

"I hope it picks up soon."

"You'll regret that. Damn it. Our entire population of eight thousand are healthy lost souls in a foreign land. Sickness for us is tweaky little infections like a cold or the flu. And we have to erase ubiquitous thoughts of suicide usually designed to be unsuccessful. My god, we get pilots and passengers with blocked eardrums—have you ever heard of blocked eardrums as a life-threatening condition?—and never any diagnosis that needs the cutting edge of medical advancement. It drives me to distraction."

Miles sat in baffled silence.

"You don't see it now. Wait a couple of weeks," Oliver said. "You'll be as disillusioned as I am."

"I'll keep alert," Miles said.

Oliver placed three books on the desk: *Larousse French-English Dictionary. Michelin Red Guide to Restaurants and Hotels. On the Genealogy of Morality.* "These are for you."

"To borrow?" Miles asked.

"A gift. These are what we came to value when we arrived."

Miles moved the books closer to look through them. "Thanks for the *Michelin Guide*," he said, "and the dictionary. I don't know French. But why Nietzsche?"

"It's from the wife. She's the intellectual. She believes we've been dumped into the remnants of the outrageous atrocities of postwar Europe. We're living with the mutilated remains of innocent humans, she thinks. Hearts grieving the extinguished lives of friends and loved ones. It's hard to ignore. She wants to know why it all happened. She's researching a book she plans to write on the Holocaust. The Aryan belief. She's all about documenting Jewish families' losses during the war. She's troubled by Nietzsche's analysis of society; she thinks it's a significant insight into the German psyche at the time. Slave and master ideas. She told me to give it to you."

Whew, Miles thought. *Nineteenth-century German philosophers.* "Thanks," he said. "I'm not sure I'll understand it."

"No one ever understands her interests in Nietzsche," Oliver said, "but she keeps handing copies to anyone near enough to accept, Jewish and non-Jewish."

Miles couldn't imagine Oliver as the philosophy type. "Have you read it?"

"Hell, no. I don't give a damn about the German psyche," Oliver said.

"Slave and master ideas?"

"Christ. It's more than that. She goes bonkers when people mention Nietzsche."

"Is it related to the camps?"

"Obliquely. She says Nietzsche believed that Western democracy was slavish and weak and that the weak would conquer the strong. He saw it as the degeneration of humankind. Those slaves-overpowering-the-masters ideas."

"Seems ponderous," Miles said.

"Moronic," Oliver said.

"But I'll give it a try. My thanks to your wife."

"Don't bother reading. Cliff's notes, maybe." Oliver shook his head in disdain. "How did triage go?" he asked.

Miles's raised eyebrows questioned Oliver's meaning.

"Your results," Oliver explained.

"I passed, but Springer seemed disappointed."

"Springer's an asshole."

"The adjutant said Springer was weird, that he hated people smarter and better trained."

"Every doc believes that," Oliver said. "But Springer's pretty damn stupid. He's disliked by everyone except for a few lackeys."

"Did he say anything to you?" Miles asked.

"He said I made it as if he expected me to fail. He's not impressed with my medical training."

"Really? Where?"

"Miami."

"What's wrong with that?"

"It's only been accredited for a few years. In Springer's mind, it's got no reputation. The school of medicine needed students, and even with me being a Jew with no top honors in college, they accepted me. I was lucky."

"Where did Springer go to med school?"

"Alabama. He'll detest your Boston education. You thought triage was valuable?"

"Not really," Miles said.

"It's the process that sucks," Oliver said. The observers aren't docs. And they don't grade the treatment of life-and-death decisions. They grade your following the rules and how fast you complete your work."

Miles shook his head. "That can't matter. In a nuclear disaster, who would be alive to respond?" he asked.

"It's ridiculous," Oliver said. "They triage victims like the wounded on the battlefield at Gettysburg. Feed them booze, saw off a limb, stop the bleeding with a hot iron."

"Death would be ubiquitous," Miles said.

"That's what Springer thinks, too," Oliver said. "But really, military docs would be the first responders. If we were alive, guys like you and me, on the periphery, we wouldn't be able to get to ground zero. There'd be no reason."

Miles shook his head in agreement.

"And even if we were alive, we haven't been trained in survival prospects, morbidity, and the delirium at the edge of nuclear disasters," Miles said.

"It's strange, isn't it. Tie on some colored armbands and they let you go by instinct from there. Let me tell you. We'll never learn anything here."

Miles winced. "The military should train us. Teach every new idea and technique. They're still studying Hiroshima and Nagasaki. It's an obligation to tell us what's been learned so far."

"Good luck with that," Oliver said.

"We ought to do something, Oliver," Miles said.

"Not really interested. It's the military's problem. Jesus, they'd fail if they took education on anyway."

"But think about what might be done," Miles said. "We could work on a strategy. It wouldn't take much time."

"Not worth any time."

"Come on. It would be good for all of us."

"Look. I'm not a crusader, Miles, and I don't want to be involved."

"It's not about a crusade. It's training."

"Let's talk about it some other time, my man. It's toxic thinking about trying to teach the military anything. In the meantime, my wife wants to have you to dinner. Tuesday night? Can you come? She's one hell of a cook."

"Where do you live?"

In Brassioux. You know where Brassioux is, don't you? Built by the military on French land. Off base. Can't tell one house from another except by the number on the door. Can you make it?"

Miles didn't hesitate. "Pleased to," he said. "Maybe I'll find a place in Brassioux, too." His first invitation.

Oliver stood. "And ditch the uniform."

Miles gave a thumbs-up as Oliver turned to leave.

***

Oliver Stern's wife turned out to be the same woman who had welcomed Miles at the airport. At first, she seemed to have forgotten their encounter entirely. His memories of their meeting precluded a too enthusiastic greeting. "Hello," he said tentatively. "Miles Ballard."

"Ingrid Stern. I'm sorry for my folly at the airport," she whispered to Miles.

Miles couldn't make his eyes stray. She had a captivating casual beauty he had not recognized previously. Dressed in a white silk blouse with pearl buttons and open at the neck, white slacks, and pumps with medium heels that made almost no sound as she glided over the wood floor; she had an unpretentious, casual elegance, the exact opposite of the ostentatious, overpriced, feminine styles in Boston. After aperitifs in the living room, they moved to a casually set dinner table in an open space off the kitchen. Ingrid served sautéed veal cutlets with fresh green beans and dauphinoise potatoes. When Miles asked about Ingrid's background, her intelligence was evident. She had degrees in art history and psychology. She had been a professional dancer in New York and now, in her early thirties, was still trim and athletic.

Oliver had grown up in Yonkers. He attended the State University of New York at Farmingdale. His father was a rabbi and his marriage to Ingrid was arranged by a *shadchan*. But he wasn't religious, Oliver made clear. In any way.

Eventually, Miles directed the lively conversation to the lack of training and the inadequacy of triage in the Air Force.

"Do you agree about the triage?" Ingrid asked her husband.

"Miles wants to change the world, Ingrid. It's bonkers," Oliver replied.

Miles put his fork and knife on the plate and wiped his mouth with his linen napkin. "Don't listen to him . . ." he began.

"I ignore him whenever possible," Ingrid smiled.

" . . . but I've thought a lot about it," Miles continued. "It's a Cold War. We're surrounded by an enemy with nuclear capabilities. We need nuclear disaster training."

"The military is an intellectual vacuum," Oliver said. "The military will do nothing."

"We deserve the training," Miles insisted.

"They make puny attempts at teaching, but they don't have a concept of postgraduate education as their responsibility," Oliver said. "They'll let anybody work at their level of incompetence until they leave the service and then just replace them with an equally incompetent or worse. They don't care about doctors like you or me. We're puppets."

Ingrid shook her head. "Miles certainly isn't Pinocchio, Ollie. He doesn't need a rebirth."

"Wait till you get to know him," Oliver laughed, glancing at Miles. "He'll wooden-salute the masters like all of us."

"You rarely salute anyone," Ingrid said.

"A slave to no one."

"See, Miles, he's read Nietzsche about masters," Ingrid said.

"I never really read it," Oliver said, "and what I skimmed I didn't understand. But docs *are* puppets in this military social structure."

"That's a little heavy for me," Miles said. "I want to improve as a doctor, do better than I did today."

"Well, it may be a little overambitious, scheming to change the training of a military environment that assumes, with invented pride, you've been adequately trained when they hire you," Oliver said.

"I was commandeered," Miles responded.

"What's your goal?" Ingrid asked.

"Right now, to convince the military to do something about preparing docs for mass casualties. Be accurate and trained to assess and minimize mortality," Miles said. "Hire experts to teach us."

"What will that do?" Ingrid asked.

"If we have training, it'll make a difference in health care by understanding disasters and using healing to advance medical research."

"Springer doesn't want doctors or staff for their education—or competence," Oliver said. "He's nepotistic, for one; he hires family as civilian workers with inflated pay. His son services vending machines in the base hospital. In the States, he hired his daughter as a not-really-needed civilian receptionist before she got married to a jerk and moved to Alaska."

"Is that permitted?" Miles asked.

"Moving to Alaska?"

"No. Nepotism," Miles replied, annoyed, becoming aware of Oliver's cynical humor.

"Absolutely. And the military has a lot of civilian jobs available everywhere."

"I know," Miles said, "but aren't there regulations?"

"I'm a civilian," Ingrid said. "Is that nepotistic?"

"A miracle you slipped through screening," Oliver chuckled. "But it's not the same, Ingrid. I didn't hire you."

"Seems to me they're lucky to have you," Miles said to Ingrid.

"The military hires women civilians who are well built as they can find and know their place," Oliver said.

"Well built?"

"In the military mentality, women are born to be domestic sex icons with parental skills," Oliver observed.

"Oliver!" Ingrid admonished.

"It's true. It's God's will."

"We need to change that attitude if we're to be successful," Miles said. "And we'd need the support of all the docs."

"They're all male," Ingrid said.

"But not all misogynists, are they?" Miles asked.

Oliver looked to Ingrid. "Tell him training is not possible."

"I think it's an admirable idea," she said emphatically. "And it's especially important for dependents, too. We're humiliated and ignored by the military. And we suffer the same threat of nuclear extinction as you do. We'd be left to die in a field of rubble after a nuclear disaster in a foreign country. Why don't you help him out, Ollie?"

Oliver shrugged. "I believe in saving your important battles for when you really need them."

"It's not a battle," Miles said, "it's a request,"

"He's right, Ollie. There's no risk of retaliation," Ingrid said. "And it *is* important. Very important."

"Neither of you knows Springer as I do," Oliver said. "And retaliations in a military community are daily occurrences."

"We could bypass Springer," Miles said. "Go to the division commander first."

"Do it, Ollie," Ingrid said. "It's not much to ask. You're not pleased with what the military does for us."

"I get agitated by thoughts of Springer," Oliver said. "He is a bastard, but he's got a lousy job."

"That doesn't make his conduct acceptable."

Oliver shook his head. "Let's change the subject. Besides, I'm still hungry."

Ingrid sighed. "You two are the worst dinner conversationalists alive," she smiled with her eyes. "Thank goodness there's more to eat."

"Will you help me?" Miles asked Oliver hesitantly.

"It seems not much to ask," Ingrid said.

Oliver shrugged compliantly. "Two against one isn't kosher. I'll give it a try. But without enthusiasm."

"Thanks," Miles said, still puzzled at Oliver's resistance to change for the better.

The thought of eating more of Ingrid's cuisine pleased everyone; she replenished as desired.

***

A few weeks later, Miles and Oliver took a developed proposal for effective triage training for medical personnel to the division commander, Dillinger. In a disaster, they pointed out, doctors and victims would clearly benefit from physician training at the triage level. Saving lives! Responding to mass casualties!

The commander seemed distracted and listened with dim interest.

"Where's Springer?" he asked.

"Sir?" Miles asked.

"Has he approved this?"

"He knows about it, sir," Miles said. "Was that necessary? Approval?"

"Jesus, he's the hospital commander."

"We weren't sure he'd support it. And there's an acute need for all hospital personnel especially," Miles said. "All the docs support us."

"That's true," Oliver added. "I'm sure he'll approve if he's approached with kid gloves."

"Listen to me very carefully," the commander said, "We're in the Air Force. There's a chain of command. You follow that chain. Involve Springer and get his approval. He's the one to present it to me."

"Could you at least give us your endorsement?" Miles asked. "That's not breaking the chain of command, is it?"

"I won't endorse it," the commander said. "I won't commit without Springer's approval. I won't undermine his authority. That's not wise in the Air Force."

"But are there alternate ways for us to succeed, sir?" Miles asked.

"You need Springer's support!"

"Yes, sir," Miles said. "We'll try. But confidentially, do you like the idea?"

The commander paused for a few seconds. "It's a good idea," he said without rancor. "But don't ever quote me."

Miles responded. "That means a lot to us, sir. We thank you. And we'll follow your directions to the letter."

Miles looked to Oliver, who had nothing to say. They stood, saluted, and left.

The next day, Miles and Oliver met with Springer.

"It's shit," Springer said. "Christ, we got a continuing-education program. We have it every month. We had a speaker from the Army a couple months ago on something. And each of you have time off to go to courses."

Only if they're on base, Miles thought. *And we're given all that anecdotal drivel about 'how I succeeded in my career.' Never valued education.* He said, "But this is an intense effort to get everyone current with developments that we don't have now, sir."

"We do damn well if you consider my budget."

"We could request money from the division commander. He might be responsive. "

"I ain't going to be indebted to him for some no-count favor. And he would never do me a favor, anyway. He doesn't give a bird poop about supporting the hospital. He's a tightass."

"But again, sir, the overall purpose is better training for triage. Better care. Increased survival. It benefits doctors and staff and, most of all, the patients and dependents."

"Triage is fine as it is," Springer said.

"And about training in general? "

"We do great. Don't be saying otherwise."

"But . . ."

"No buts. That's all."

"We're sorry, sir," Oliver said in an apologetic tone. Miles remained silent.

"Don't let it happen again," Springer said.

Miles's irritation left him at a loss for words. It took a full five seconds before he and Oliver stood to leave.

Late in the afternoon the next day, as Miles walked down the corridor toward his exam room, Oliver caught up with him. "You look down, my man. What's eating you?"

"It's being the General's personal physician. It can't be a rewarding job."

"I've heard that's an assignment many have wiggled out of.'"

"I tried. Springer said it was an order."

"Sorry, man," Oliver said. "You need a break. You been to the Bumpy Landing yet?"

Miles shook his head no.

"It's for officers. Private. Members only. In Déols, away from Châteauroux and the base. I'll drive," Oliver said, "and I'll introduce you as a potential member. I'm thinking of investing as a part-owner soon and they need new members."

"The Bumpy Landing?"

"A place for officers to relax outside the military, among their own. Privately run by a retired NCO who didn't want to return to the States, Patrick O'Leary. Everyone calls him Paddy. It's like a civilian gentleman's club. No women. Uniforms not required. No sign on the door. Rank matters. And real private. It's a gentleman's paradise, and no member discusses it, even when pressed, with anyone not a member. So, keep a zipped lip. You get it?"

Miles nodded.

"You up for a little refreshment?" Oliver asked. "We could stay for a meal if you're not busy."

Miles nodded.

"After today," Miles said, "it's a dream come true."

"I can put you up for membership tomorrow. Fifty to join. Fifteen bucks a month dues. I can get you letters of endorsement. Docs always get in."

Obviously, Oliver was a smooth character. A social magnet, too. But Miles wasn't sure about the club. It wasn't really his style.

They were at the Bumpy Landing at the polished walnut bar, seated on carved wooden stools with red leather seats. They faced a life-size oil painting behind the bar, between two wide cabinets, each with glass-paned doors with four shelves filled with sparkling clean glasses.

"You like that?" Oliver asked, pointing to the gold-leaf-framed artwork.

Miles gazed at the canvas. A life-size, sleeping, nubile nude lay on a chaise lounge draped with a gray coverlet trimmed in silver. A white sheet barely covered her right upper thigh and pudendum. A meticulously placed, dainty-white silk wrap covered her neck and right arm but did nothing to obscure any part of her upper anatomy or any of the sulking sensuality of the sleeping pose.

"Incredible, isn't it?" Oliver asked.

"Who did it?" Miles asked.

"Christ, I don't know." Oliver raised his hand for the bartender's attention. "Charlie. Who painted this babe?"

"Local artist, sir. It's a copy of *Sleeping Nude* by Gustave Courbet."

Oliver smiled. "Hey, not bad. Even a French guy in the boondocks can arouse a guy. Right?" He turned to Miles. "What you going to do, my man? Springer squashed us like roaches on a concrete floor."

"Why is Springer so Springerish?" Miles asked.

"He's evil, Miles. Vindictive to the core. You'd be crazy to carry the triage thing too far. Springer sees anything done in the hospital that he didn't initiate as insubordination."

"Insubordination?"

"It's military weird. Any slight, any innuendo, any contradiction of an order, any action taken without a superior's knowing what's going on can be interpreted as insubordination. The chain of command has precedence over logic or reason. I've heard Springer say it many times. He hates insubordination."

"But we made a reasonable proposal."

"Not me, my man. It was yours all the way. I was there to support *you*, not the document."

"You don't support the proposal?"

"I've got nothing against it. It's just not important to me—not worth any risk to my career for supporting it."

"So what would Springer actually do?"

"You never know."

"How can he think a proposal to provide education for his staff is insubordination? It has nothing to do with him."

"I tell you, in the military mindset anything that reflects in any way on the career or the impression of a superior officer is a punishable offense. Court-martial. And any penalty except death."

"Even if a proposal has validity?"

"If it appears you're disobeying your commanding officer, you're guilty. Makes no difference if what is done or said is the truth, or valuable, or morally correct. If there's a perceived hint of disobedience, the accused is guilty of insubordination. It's not that often. But it happens."

"Would he do that to me?"

"He would. But I don't think it's worth his time right now. And probably not for a proposal for postgraduate education. You got time before dinner? There's someone I'd like you to meet."

Miles shrugged. "Sure."

They walked behind the bar to a room layered with smoke from card players at four tables. A room with three pool tables was visible to their left. They entered the kitchen, saturated with the diffuse aromas of food in preparation. Patrick O'Leary was there—a short man with blue eyes and a full reddish beard talking to a chef in a toque.

They went outside through a side door and walked single file down a narrow alley and turned right on a narrow street to enter a three-story house, then straight through and out the back. They went to the iron fire escape at the side of an adjacent house, away from street views, and climbed to the top floor. Inside, after a knock on an apartment door, they were greeted by an attractive woman in a terrycloth robe cinched at the waist. Her untethered black hair touched her shoulders, and her dark brown eyes held a penetrating but distant gaze. Her attractive, refined smile lacked any disclosure of her feelings. Oliver introduced Miles.

"Captain Ballard, this is Michelle," Oliver said. "She pretty much runs this place. You got to be a member, and you need Paddy's approval to get in." As they walked back into the bar at the Bumpy Landing to have dinner, Oliver said, "Michelle's really a gem. Kind, discreet. Sort of the mother for the girls."

"How did she wind up here?"

"Many French women consorted with the enemy during the war. Some voluntarily, I'm sure, but most had lost husbands, had kids, no job. Sometimes they were raped, other times, they didn't resist in order to survive on pay of a few French coins. Christ, there are more than two hundred thousand children in France today born from Germans and collaborators screwing vulnerable French women."

"Do you think Michelle was forced by circumstances?"

"Maybe. We'll never know. But I've seen photos. She was humiliated in public after liberation. The resistance shaved her head and marched her through the community as a horizontal collaborator with the enemy."

"Terrible," Miles said. "But why support the Nazis?"

"To survive. Don't think ill of her. She's all gold," Oliver said.

"Thanks," Miles said, but he couldn't help thinking that upholding prostitution was something he would never do, married or single. *How much does Ingrid know about the Bumpy Landing?* he thought. *And it's not just an officer's club with drinks and bar food, gambling and shooting pool. It's prostitution. I wish I'd never heard of the place.* He thanked Oliver for the invitation to join and said he'd consider it. But it still didn't appeal to him, and he doubted he'd apply.

"Mum's the word," Oliver said.

CHAPTER 4
The General

1960
Miles

As a base commander, Brigadier General Thomas Read was more figurehead than leader. His staff tolerated him, but with minimal respect, and they spent their careers making essential decisions for him based solely on their knowledge and skills. The General, now sixty-five, labored under insuppressible delusions of an early death, inspired by a series of heart flutters suffered in his forties.

On first examination of the General, and reviewing his medical record, Miles noted, "atrial fibrillation."

"I know that! I didn't deserve it," the General said.

"You were treated well, sir?"

"Of course, I was! Walter Reed for chrissakes! But they said it might come back."

Miles hesitated. He didn't dislike the General and wanted to assure him without raising yet more anxious concern—the persistent dread of all neurotics.

"You've had no symptoms for thirty years," Miles said. "Your overall health is good. The possibility of a recurrence is really very low."

"You're just out of school, aren't you?" the General demanded.

"I'm well trained, sir. At the best schools. I spent two years as a director of a research laboratory. And then I completed a rigorous internship."

"You finished, didn't you?"

"Yes, sir. Thanks to the Berry Plan I was allowed to fully train as an MD. When I finish my tour, I'll return to a surgery residency for specialization."

"Think about staying in the military, my boy. It's a good life."

Miles hesitated, "Of course, sir, I'll definitely consider it."

"Keep up with my staff; they take my blood pressure three times a day. Keep my supply of pills up to date. And schedule an EKG six times a year, hear?"

"All will be taken care of, sir," Miles said.

"And when we travel, take all that's necessary to keep me alive."

"Yes, sir. I'll be prepared."

"You take care of my family, too. My wife and two daughters. The best docs. You hear?"

"Yes, sir. Thank you, sir."

***

On his first trip with the General, Miles was headed to Israel to deliver parts for new military aircraft being developed. Parade dress required. The passenger seats installed in front of the cargo hold on the C-118 were half full. Miles recognized the General, an attaché, an adjutant, and two NCOs, but no one else.

"Hey, Ballard, come here," the General said. He told an attractive woman in uniform in her early thirties sitting next to him to take another seat. Miles buckled up next to the General, and they remained quiet until after the climb-out to cruising altitude, and the four-engine roar abated.

"You married?" the General asked Miles.

"No, sir. I hope to be someday. Have a family. "

"Stay single, boy. Stay focused on your duty. Women distract good men from their assignments."

"What is my duty on this trip, sir?"

"You don't know?"

"No one's told me."

"See. That's what I mean about keeping focused. You won't be any damn good unless you've got the gumption to find out what's needed, what's going on. You gotta find things out."

"Yes, sir. And what should I be doing today?"

"Jesus, Ballard. Talk to the lawyer Goggin. He's over there."

"Yes, sir," Miles said. *Has he forgotten why he called me over?* But the General started talking, poking Miles with unneeded force on the arm.

"And when you're on your own on these trips, keep in communications with the adjutant every few hours. And look sharp!"

"Yes, sir."

"Talk to these passengers here. You'll depend on all of them to get your duty right."

"Yes, sir. And thank you, sir." *I guess that's all.*

"Tell Patricia to come back and sit here," the General said.

Miles signaled Patricia and went to where the lawyer, Bob Goggin, was seated.

"I'm the General's physician," Miles said. "Miles Ballard."

"Lucky you."

"You're not happy?"

Goggin leaned closer to Miles and lowered his voice. "I'm miserable."

"Why?"

"I'm a slave to the General's ego. He's a wannabe dictator without a plan. And a lousy leader."

"Why do you put up with it?"

"You're not regular, are you?"

"Going back to complete my surgical training after the tour."

"Where?"

"Charity Hospital in New Orleans. LSU service. It's a great place for surgery."

"Well, I'm stuck, man. I'm twelve years to early retirement. Then bingo. Out of here."

"So what am I supposed to do on these trips?"

"It's ridiculous. When they can arrange it, staff gets local dignitaries to meet the General."

"Why?"

"It's not logical. It's not like it's going to boost international relations or admiration for Americans. It's to give the General a ceremony. He loves ceremonies."

"And what do *we* do?"

"We stand at the end of the airplane stairs, in two lines of you, me, and the General's staff and flunkies, and we wait for his highness to emerge at the top of the flight steps when the dignitaries arrive at the plane. Then the General descends, ramrod straight, slowly, with faux dignity, and we salute until he's on the ground."

"This is your career?" Miles asked.

"It gets worse. With a forced smile, he shakes hands with the dignitaries and chats with anyone he thinks is important enough to deserve his time. Always in English, and few foreign dignitaries understand him. Meanwhile, we're still standing at attention. And if you're not sharp, he'll give you demerits. So he introduces us each as his physician, his lawyer, his nurse, his pilot, his copilot, and the like. When he's finished, the adjutant steps out in front of us all, salutes, and yells, 'Dismissed.'"

"*Then* what do I do?"

"We do what we want on this one. We wander off. We're here overnight and leave tomorrow before noon. Not much time, but there's a squash court near the barracks. Do you play?"

"In college. But I don't have the gear."

"They'll lend you a racquet and clothes."

"And a place to shower?"

"Of course. And a grill for food and drinks."

"I'd like to play," Miles said.

"Well, good. Take it easy on me, I'm not worth a shit. And my feelings are hurt when I lose."

"I'll play left-handed."

"You're a real gentleman. Are you right-handed?"

"I'll never tell."

"Ambidextrous, eh?"

"I guarantee one hand is better than the other."

"Twenty bucks each to the pot. Winner takes all," Goggin said, grinning.

Miles had never played squash for money. "You hustler," he said.

"Second only to you," Goggin replied.

CHAPTER 5

Engagement

1960
Miles

Two days later, Miles had dinner again at Ingrid and Oliver's. When they'd finished eating, Ingrid suggested they sit outside to watch the sunset and have dessert and wine.

"I'll get the table and chairs," Oliver said.

"Open a bottle of the Barsac, please, Ollie," Ingrid requested.

"Late vintage Sauterne from Bordeaux," Oliver said to Miles. "A dessert wine. Give it a try?"

"I'd like to," Miles said, becoming more eager to try wines and catch the lingo of aficionados.

"Show Miles your paintings," Oliver said.

Ingrid led Miles through the house pointing out oil paintings on the walls of every room—flower arrangements, farm scenes, sunsets, townscapes, bucolic settings. He found the work engaging and pleasing.

"I like them," he said. "Have you been painting long?"

"In school mostly. I took painting seriously when we arrived in France. I hope to find a teacher."

Back in the kitchen, Ingrid took three desserts made with custard and meringue from the refrigerator. "*Île flottante*," she said. "I learned from a cooking class in town."

She carried two bowls and handed one to Miles. "Open the door for me, please," she said.

Oliver had set up three iron chairs around a small, yellow-painted wooden table on the carefully tended lawn. As the sun approached the horizon, the light began to fade; the green of the lawn and the vibrant flowers and shrubs so carefully planted in a garden plot near the house darkened to a leaden gray.

"You know, there's a chill," Ingrid said a few minutes later. "Let's move to the family room."

Ingrid placed lit candles on the mantle and side tables. After Oliver served Calvados in brandy glasses, he settled with Ingrid on a two-seater overstuffed sofa. Miles sat in a matching armchair.

"Have you ever been married, Miles?" Ingrid asked.

"Sorry, my man, she's a card-carrying romantic," Oliver said.

"I tried," said Miles, impressed and a little envious of the warm, caring reciprocity he saw between Ingrid and Oliver, that his story would seem parched and ordinary. He'd decided to move on to other topics when Ingrid said, "So, tell us! How did you meet?"

Her interest, tinted with concern, touched him. He needed to tell someone, to judge their reactions.

"The elite women's society groups in Boston have fairs on the Boston Commons to provide food and clothing for the homeless. Medical students are asked to volunteer to do exams if needed. I saw her . . ."

"She was a socialite?"

"Yes. Rich and related; she claimed—as many citizens in Boston do—to have blood relations to the Cabots and the Lodges. Who knows? I found her so attractive I asked her out to dinner at the Parker House hotel on our first meeting."

"Did she live in Boston?"

"Her family's house was on Beacon Hill, but she was there only when school was out. She worked in admissions at Smith College a hundred miles north in Northampton. When we did get together, it was always in Boston and only for a couple of days. We usually went to the Museum of Fine Arts and never missed a Hatch Shell concert. She didn't enjoy the Bruins or Red Sox games I took her to. Twice we went out to Provincetown for parades, and many times to Tanglewood festival events."

"It seems so idyllic," Ingrid said. "What happened?"

"So, I bought this engagement ring from Shreve, Crump, and Low, the most expensive jeweler in Boston. A carat-and-a-half diamond set in white gold. But when I offered it to her, she shoved it away. 'Have you asked Daddy?' she asked. I said I could call him, but she said no, it had to be in person. He's traditional. 'They're in Maine,' she said. They had retired there and were having a family get-together on Saturday. 'You can stay in the attic,' she said.

"I put the ring back in the jewelry box and offered it to her again. 'It will be a secret commitment between us.' But she said to keep it and bring it with me. 'Can't we go together?' I asked. But she was going up Thursday with Aunt Eunice. She turned to leave. 'I've got to go to Filene's to find a dress for commencement.'"

Oliver refreshed the brandy glasses.

"So, what happened in Maine?" Ingrid asked.

"It didn't start well. The weekenders who crowded I-95 held me up in traffic at the New Hampshire border. I arrived an hour and a half late. Emily was out walking along the coast with her Aunt Eunice.

"I introduced myself to the family and their friends. No one seemed to be aware of my feelings for Em, and no one seemed to know exactly who I was. I was thankful when Em entered the room with her hair tousled from the ever-present offshore winds, her delicate skin pinked rosy by the sun. Her natural beauty always astonished me. Without a word, she led me outside to her father who tended a brick grill in the lee of the house behind sharp-edged stone boulders that protected from the weather. After a hug and a brief greeting with her father, she left me on my own."

"Was he what you expected?" Oliver asked.

"For the most part. He wore a full white apron emblazoned with this sketchy, age-faded image of James Beard. He prodded steaks with one hand and flipped aluminum-foil-wrapped baked potatoes gripped by stainless-steel tongs with the other. 'I'd like to marry Em,' I finally said, faking confidence and sounding totally inadequate."

"'Your idea?'"

"'We'd both like your permission, sir. It's important to both of us.'"

Lodge stoked the charcoal fire and he signaled to a black servant who stood at the door at the back of the house to take over tending the grill.

"'Walk the coastline with me,' Lodge said. 'We need to talk.'"

"We walked side by side on a narrow path that spiraled among the rocks. 'I appreciate your time to be able . . .' I began. 'Don't grovel,' Lodge interrupted. 'Talk straight.'"

"I adjusted my stride to his measured, slower pace."

"'And you've already asked her, haven't you?'"

"'Yes,' I said."

"'It's a little late to come to me, then.'"

"'I got here as soon as possible,' I countered. 'Em was upset that I hadn't asked you first, sir. She didn't want to make a commitment until I talked with you.'"

"'I am upset. I expect a wannabe son-in-law to follow convention. It's lust, isn't it? Your generation is always about getting a great lay.'"

"'Not at all,' I said, offended by the implication. I was sure Emily was a virgin. At least she'd claimed to be when avoiding any serious intimacy."

"'Your generation scorns etiquette,' Lodge said. He stopped walking abruptly, standing silently, staring at the sea. I told him again, 'It's not lust. We're in love!' Lodge- scoffed. 'What do you have to offer her?' I was ready for that. 'I hope for a very happy existence. I'm a doctor with every chance of a successful career.'"

"'You went to Harvard?' he asked. I told him Tufts for medical school, Boston City Hospital for my internship."

"I'd really begun to dislike Lodge by this point."

"Lodge stared at the sea as we began walking again. 'What do your parents do?' he asked."

"My father drove his own long-haul, eighteen-wheeler until he retired. And he made handcrafted furniture to sell. My mother taught preschoolers. My father died a few years ago. My mother's been in terminal care with dementia for more than a decade. She doesn't recognize anyone now, not even family. My two sisters care for her.'"

"Lodge said that made him even more concerned. 'I wonder if you're qualified to keep Emily in the manner she is accustomed to.'

Of course, he meant Emily's social status, club memberships, appointments, and potential leadership in political and charitable Boston institutions. I said I'd be a good husband. Lodge raised his voice over the sound of the surge on the rocks. 'How can you know that?' he said."

"'I love your daughter as no one else will.'"

"'I don't think that's true,' he responded. 'She is adored by everyone.'"

"'Do you approve of our engagement?'"

"'I don't know yet,' he said. I told him 'I'll be meeting my service obligation in a few months.'"

"He frowned. 'Vietnam?'"

"'No, France. I'd like to take Emily with me as my wife.'"

"'She loves Boston, my boy. Wait till you return to ask.'"

"'We'd like to start our new life together . . . as soon as possible.'"

"'And you think being a military wife in France is decent for a girl like Em?' he asked belligerently."

"'Of course!' I said.

Lodge glanced toward the house. 'I'll see what Mrs. Lodge thinks.'"

"That night at ten o'clock, Em showed me to the narrow, cramped stairs to the attic. The walls angled sharply to a peak and a single, small, triangular-shaped window provided a narrow view to the sea but allowed only a modicum of light to filter in. I switched on the bare, sixty-watt bulb dangling from the ceiling by a black electrical cord. A cot without linens or pillow was tucked into the wedge made by the ceiling with the floor. I lay down fully dressed and pulled up an antique quilt that would have barely covered a child. I used my rolled-up coat for a pillow. An hour later, I heard Emily's parents talking in their bedroom directly below. They were preparing for bed. Minutes later, Lodge asked his wife something I couldn't make out. The light switch clicked off."

"'I told her no,' Em's mom said. 'Parker desires her.'"

"'My God, Parker is crazy only for himself.'"

"'Lodge asked his wife what Em had said.'"

"'Mrs. Lodge said that "She doesn't want Parker."'"

"'That's understandable!'"

"'Not at all, Calvin. She should learn to care for him over time and she would be content with him in every way.' Her tone was distorted and angry."

"'You don't like this Ballard boy, do you?' Lodge said."

"'He is not one of us, Calvin,' Mrs. Lodge said."

"'Do you think she loves him?'"

"'Of course not. She's infatuated, for chrissakes. And she's too well bred to be sidetracked by romance.'"

"'If she loves him . . .'"

"'She doesn't love him! She doesn't have the capacity. And she's got Parker!'"

"'He's too old, Brenda. He'd be like a stepfather.'"

"'Well, she doesn't love this boy, whatever his name is.'"

"'Miles, his name is Miles,' he said. She snorted."

"'He's got no connections.'"

"'Well, Parker has connections but he's not likable. Or lovable. And if she loves the boy, we could introduce him to those that matter.'"

"'He'd sink like a stone dropped into the ocean. He's not her type. She deserves someone who's comfortable in life, who would make her life royal.'"

"'Let her make the decision, Brenda. I'm sure the boy would support her.'"

"'He's a doctor, for god's sake. His time and his brain are taken by others.'"

"That pissed me off a bit."

"Lodge continued, 'That's not fair, Brenda.'"

"'Name me one doctor we know whose wife is happy. Just one! Doctors marry women who are like their aides, or receptionists, or loyal cooks. Thoughtless slaves.'"

"Lodge said it still should be Em's choice, but she said, 'Doctors are too busy working on their Humpty Dumpties.'"

"'What if she accepts without our blessing?'"

"'God forbid. We'll cut her off.'"

"'We can't do that.'"

"'Don't worry, she hasn't got the gumption to go against us.'"

"Hours later, still awake and thinking about what had been said,

I heard snorts and wheezes. I couldn't stay in the house any longer. At just past three o'clock, I descended the stairs, left the box with the ring on the dining room table, and walked to my car. I wiped a thin layer of ice from the windshield, and left. Three and a half hours later, I was back in Boston. For three days, Emily did not return my repeated calls until finally she left a message on my answering machine to meet her in Boston Garden."

"She greeted me without touching and suggested we sit on a bench on a path near the bridge over the pond with the swan boats. I still had hope things would go my way."

"In the midst of gaiety and excitement in the crowd, we were encased in an awkward silence. I tried to be upbeat. 'Your house in Maine is really impressive,' I said. But all she said was, 'Why did you leave without thanking my parents?' I took a deep breath. 'I heard them talking in their bedroom, Em. It wasn't pleasant.'"

"'You were spying!'"

"'No. Of course not. I could hear everything clear as day from the attic.'"

"'It's bad-mannered.'"

"'Really, I couldn't help but hear. Your mother definitely doesn't like me. Your father thought you should make your own decision. I thought that was decent of him.'"

"'It's hard for them, Miles. We talked about it for hours.'"

"'Why is it hard?' 'They want me to marry Parker Batten!' 'Only your mother?' 'No, both of them.' I doubted that."

"'Did they tell you I don't measure up to their standards?' She stared with a strange, lifeless agitation at a swan boat filled to capacity, then took out the ring box from her bag and handed it to me. Now she looked impatient with restless irritation and did not look at me. 'I can't accept this,' she said. I told her I loved her, but she said she'd accepted Parker's proposal and that she had to go. I asked her to wait, but she said it was over, and that she was frankly glad to have made a decision. Then she told me not to follow her and walked away."

"With an almost empty wine glass, I reached out to Oliver for a refill. I had always believed if two people really loved one another, nothing could keep them apart."

"'Damn women,' Oliver said."

"Ingrid frowned at Oliver. 'I'm so sorry, Miles. Will you ever get over her?'"

"'I don't know,' I said. 'Maybe with time, but I doubt it.' The whole affair erased my confidence with women. I wasn't the right guy for her, that's for certain, but the real folly was that for two years, I thought she loved me."

CHAPTER 6
Alyce

New York City
Late 1961
Alyce

Alyce Read wrote weekly articles on cuisine and culture for the *New York Herald Tribune*. For years, the troubled paper dealt with strikes and changes in leadership and Alyce dreaded this emergency meeting with purpose undisclosed. After two hours of waiting, a secretary told her she could enter.

Jacob Heinemann, the editor-in-chief, sat behind a desk cluttered with papers and books, a typewriter, and a dial phone. Months-old holiday-gift wrappings spilled out of a trash can at the side of his desk. He hadn't shaved in days and his dark brown eyes were dimmed with fatigue.

He was not one for small talk. "Look," he said, "I don't feel good about doing this, Alyce, but I've got to let you go."

Alyce swallowed, struck by a sudden surge of anxiety. "Why?"

"The paper's folding. It's about the end for all of us."

"Couldn't you keep me on at a reduced salary for a while?" Alyce asked.

"I can't. We're rarely publishing anything on cuisine or culture now."

"Help me get a job at the *Times*, then, Jake," she said, hoping she didn't sound like she was pleading. "And I could cover culture."

"I've tried for others," Heinemann said. "It's no use. You can apply on your own, but they said to stop sending people over."

"What about the *International Tribune*?"

"Even if they wanted you, you'd have to live in Europe."

"Do they have a spot open?"

"I don't know. I doubt they're hiring."

"But I *can* live in Europe. I have family there now."

"It's a different world after the war."

"I could freelance. Get paid by the piece."

Jacob leaned back in his swivel chair and clasped his hands behind his head, breathing through his mouth. His upper lip twitched irregularly, and he wiped spit from his mouth with the back of his hand. Alyce waited, her pulse on the fly.

Considering his words carefully, Heinemann leaned forward in a gesture of intimacy. He genuinely liked Alyce and her journalism was improving. "I'll try, Alyce. I'll ask for freelance work. But to get published at all, you'd have to know Europe inside and out. And submit. I doubt you'll get assignments, at least at first."

Alyce exhaled. "I'll do it," she said. She wanted to hug him.

"I'll be in touch, then. But I don't think there's much chance they'll buy it."

But they did accept, with reluctance. The editor in Paris told Alyce she needed to improve her writing, but based on Heinemann's recommendation, he'd let her freelance as long as she understood it was for a trial period.

***

Three weeks later, Alyce arrived in France, where her father, Brigadier General Thomas Read, base commander of the Châteauroux air base, and her mother, Gertrude, lived in the American-constructed housing development of Brassioux. Alyce contemplated their single-family, one-story house painted a pale, dirt-puddle brown with faded off-white trim around doors and windows.

Her mother expected her arrival but was far less cordial than Alyce had hoped. "The General is in Berlin," her mother said. "I think he'll be back tomorrow. He's always gone these days with the Cold War." Alyce guessed her father's absences were less due to a General's duties and more to escape her mother's doom-and-gloom personality, spiced with acid critiques of everything and everybody.

Her mother directed Alyce to carry her luggage to a bedroom at the back of the house. "I've made macaroni and cheese for tonight. Your favorite!"

Not since I was nine, Alyce thought, immediately sorry for mentally reproving her mother so soon after her arrival.

The only furniture in the bedroom was a single bed with folded linen, a pillow without a case, a wadded-up military-issue blanket on the mattress, and a metal folding chair.

"Do you have a table for a typewriter?" Alyce asked.

"I'll have to requisition a table. It always takes a while. You'll have to buy a typewriter from the commissary."

"Could I use the dining room table until the table arrives?"

"I'll give you a tablecloth to protect the surface."

Alyce asked mother if they could explore the base before she prepared dinner. But mother didn't drive in France, and she wouldn't let Alyce drive their car without the General's permission.

"I'll unpack," Alyce said.

"You can read in the living room until dinner, dear."

"That's fine, Mother, but I think I'll take a walk."

"Tommy's arranged a tour for you with a captain's wife after you've settled a little. Her name is Ingrid something. She works for development as a paid guide for newcomers."

The General never did make it home, and Alyce and her mother ate alone. Alyce went to bed to read, but the only light filtering from an opaque-white glass domed-fixture on the ceiling was too meager to read by. She lay, discouraged, staring up at two flies creeping erratically where the ceiling met the wall until she fell asleep.

***

Almost two weeks after Alyce's arrival, Ingrid and Alyce left the base for a day trip to the Château de Chinon. Alyce declined to ride in Ingrid's staff car and insisted on driving the General's Citroën DS for practice on French roads. Ingrid sat in the passenger seat with a Michelin map of central France laid out on her lap. They started on the D943 heading northwest.

"Your husband's a doctor?" Alyce asked.

"Yes, an MD."

"Does he like the military?"

Ingrid looked up from the map and leaned her head back against the headrest. "He seems to," she said.

"And you?" Alyce asked.

"I really like living in France," Ingrid said, evasively.

"And the military?"

"It's okay," Ingrid said.

"Really? That doesn't sound convincing. And don't worry about me; the General may be my father, but I'm definitely not pro-military. I'm really just interested now in a possible article regarding military medicine."

"Military medicine is hard for doctors," Ingrid admitted.

"Why's that?"

"They like most of the hospital staff; it's the quality of care that bothers them. The equipment's antiquated. All the specialties aren't covered. And there's very little postgraduate education. Do you know Colonel Springer?"

"Not at all," Alyce said.

"He's the head of the hospital. Most of the doctors don't like him."

"My father thinks his hospital runs like a Swiss watch," Alyce said.

"Is that a general's perspective?"

"That's possible. Father's prone to say that things are perfect rather than try to make them better."

"How did he get to be a general?" Ingrid asked, then made an internal grimace; it was an inappropriate question.

Alyce laughed. "You don't necessarily advance in the military by hard work and distinguished skills. For many, it's mostly contacts and longevity," she said with a touch of spite.

"But he's your father."

"He's always the general to me. I can't say he considers me anything like a blood relative. Most of the time he just ignores me. He's not worthy of my admiration."

Ingrid thought for a moment, puzzled by Alyce's resentment. "You don't care for your father, then?"

Alyce laughed uneasily. "It's . . . ahh . . ."

"I'm sorry. It's rude to ask," Ingrid said hurriedly.

"He's okay, I guess," Alyce said. "He tolerates me."

"You have siblings?"

"Yes. A sister. I was adopted when I was four, three years before they conceived my sister. The General's disappointment in me made him fertile, I guess. Or maybe my mother was fruitless until then. Who knows? But my mother's definitely not the type to be unfaithful. Just incapable of making it happen for a while—or since."

"Sounds miserable."

"More like irritating. My sister Margaret is the holy grail to them. When she's around, I just feel invisible in a family consumed by self. It used to wither my self-confidence. But I'm doing better now. This is the first time I've seen my parents for more than a few days at a time in over fifteen years."

"Look out!" Ingrid cried out as they rounded a sharp curve.

Alyce slammed on the brakes and swerved to miss a two-wheeled wooden cart, loaded with logs, pulled by two brown oxen. Ingrid's head hit the dashboard. The Citroën's engine stalled and the car came to a stop, tilted into a shallow ditch. Ingrid moaned.

"Damn," Alyce muttered. "Are you hurt?"

Ingrid sat up and touched a sore spot.

"I don't see any blood," Alyce said. "But I bet there's a going to be swelling."

"I'll live," Ingrid groaned. But her head hurt.

The cart stopped a few yards in front of them. The driver, in coveralls and a long-sleeved collared shirt, cap in hand, tapped on the Citroën driver's-side window, his face contorted with distress.

Alyce rolled down the window. "We're all right," she said.

The man was close to tears and repeated over and over in French that he was sorry.

"It's okay. It was my fault," Alyce said. He seemed to know her meaning.

After Alyce and Ingrid checked the car and found no damage, Alyce started the engine and eased the Citroën back onto the road. The man smiled and waved as they pulled around the cart.

The swelling on Ingrid's forehead had turned purple. "You're sure you're all right?" Alyce asked.

"Okay," Ingrid said. "Just a little sore."

"I'm so sorry."

"Not your fault, Alyce."

"I should have been paying more attention."

After a few minutes, their heart rates slowed, and their minds calmed. Ingrid said her head felt much better. But the wound still looked painful to Alyce and she drove at a reduced speed.

"Does Oliver have any friends at the hospital?" Alyce asked.

"Miles Ballard is his best friend. He's the General's GMO."

"What's that?"

"General Medical Officer."

"He's my father's doctor?"

"Yes."

"There's nothing wrong with father. He's a health nut, and he fears death as his greatest enemy. So, as the General's physician, your friend is my doctor too?"

"I assume so. You'll be pleased. Miles is ten times smarter than anyone else at the hospital. Boston trained. Number one in his graduating class, I think. AOA. Valedictorian. And he's got a kind heart."

"Just as long as he's competent, cute, and single."

Ingrid smiled. "You'll like him. He wanted to marry this woman from Boston."

"It didn't work out?"

"Her family was from colonial times. Deep pockets. She turned him down. He was hurt."

"Probably only a few eligible boys in Boston are in her stratosphere as possibilities."

"He thought they were in love, but he wasn't from the privileged classes."

"I suspect any Boston-society girl is too full of herself to truly fall in love with anyone. Boston's that way most of the time. I went to BU. I would guess Miles would have been the first serious normal male without excessive wealth to take a sincere interest in her, and no doubt her family wouldn't like anyone not genetically tied to them. You'd have to be a weird human being to drivel in awe at Boston lineage. It's all so trivial."

"He overheard the parents talking about him. Her mother really disliked him. He told us all the details."

"You must know him well. Doctors seem so impenetrable to me. A clam in its shell."

"I know what you mean. But I think Miles is sincere, if a little reticent."

They were approaching Noyant de Touraine.

"Let's have an early lunch," Alyce said.

"Super," said Ingrid. "And on me. The General's staff has a special fund for me to entertain certain people I ferry around." She'd forgotten for the moment that Alyce was the General's daughter.

"I'm amazed at the military perks. All on the taxpayer," Alyce said.

"Well, let's not economize today," Ingrid grinned.

"Look for something in the *Michelin Guide*. In the glove compartment. Something tasty enough that I might be able to send an article to *The Tribune*."

Ingrid looked for a restaurant. "La Ciboulette looks good. It's on the route."

They ordered specialties and sauvignon blanc.

"I read last night about Château de Chinon," Alyce said.

"Where?"

"At the base library," Alyce said. "The General doesn't read books. Mother has stacks of *Ladies' Home Journal* and the *National Geographic* in the utility room, but I've never seen her reading them."

"Joan of Arc stayed at Chinon," Ingrid said. "She was burned at the stake."

They were delayed by a small herd of meandering cows, unresponsive to the young farm boy with a stick trying to manage them.

"Sort of enviable," Alyce said, "to make that much of a historical impact in just nineteen years. I'm thirty-one, willfully childless, and the lines on my CV are less than four inches, single-spaced, on one page."

"But you change people with your writing," Ingrid said.

"Any impact I have," Alyce said, "lasts less than a day. Do you write?"

"I try," Ingrid said. "I'm preparing to write about Jewish families in Europe. Not just to tell what happened during the Holocaust but to understand why it happened, and how it felt."

"I wish I were that ambitious," Alyce said.

"Many in my family died," Ingrid continued. "But we've never known the details."

"They lived in France?"

"We're sure most of my family did. Probably others in my husband's family in Germany and Poland."

"Are you writing fiction?" Alyce asked.

"Not really. More like historical fiction based on fact," Ingrid said.

"But not nonfiction? A documentary?"

"I want to make the story a tribute to those who lived it. Facts will be hard to validate. It was such a turbulent time. I'll have to rely on memories, innuendo, photos. Historical fiction seems the most effective way to capture the terror and pain of the occupation."

"That's a lot."

"Would you read it?"

"Of course," Alyce said as she slowed for a crossroads. "Are we close?"

Ingrid looked for a road sign to give an indication of their position then studied the map. "I'd guess less than twenty minutes."

The Château de Chinon dated from the tenth century and consisted of three castles and many towers. It had endured long periods of alternating grandeur and decay over many centuries. They took a tour in English led by an elderly French male guide with graying hair, shrewd blue eyes, a wry smile, and a full nut-brown beard. They were in the Tour du Coudray, the westernmost castle.

"This is where Joan of Arc stayed in 1429," the guide said. He detailed how she convinced the soon-to-be King Charles VII of the truth of her heavenly visitations. "He provided her with an army. She was victorious in many campaigns, including a momentous victory at Orléans that repulsed the English attempt to conquer France during the Hundred Years War. In 1430, she was captured and sold to the English. In Rouen, she was accused of heresy for her rejection of church authority in favor of direct inspiration from God and burned at the stake at the age of nineteen. She was canonized in 1909, and immediately became one of France's most revered saints."

The first few minutes of the drive back to Châteauroux were spent in quiet contemplation.

"That really moved me," Alyce finally said. "How hard life was. All the death and suffering. They never had a touch of joy about anything but religion, and that was more fear and guilt than joy and salvation. And they had little education, and only a dry-leaf love for a God they could barely imagine. They rarely knew true love for another, never experienced romance. Hard work and fighting for survival were all they knew."

"I wonder what scholars in a thousand years will think of us," Ingrid said. "Will they understand what being human meant to us?"

"They'll have the knowledge of a lot more philosophers and historians."

"Journalists and scientists," Ingrid agreed.

"Politicians," Alyce continued, "industrialists, and the intensely religious worshippers, all recording for those who survive to learn about us."

"But will they be able to convey what really goes on in our lives?"

"They'll have more than we know about the fifteenth century."

"But of any value for really understanding humanity?"

"I don't think anyone can understand that. Why we're here and what makes us do what we do will always be enigmas. Humanity is constantly evolving, but understanding the whys of existence is static. It's difficult to write about."

"Is understanding the past better for you?"

"For the worse, I think, now. Especially being in Europe after the war."

Ingrid smiled. When they'd first met, Alyce seemed removed from the world, like an image in a mirror, nothing more than a reflection. But she felt human to her now, and Ingrid liked her more.

CHAPTER 7
Searching for Truth

Oradour-sur-Glane
1961
Ingrid

On Saturday morning after rounds, Miles waited in front of the hospital as Ingrid and Oliver approached in their Jaguar sedan. He drove; Ingrid sat in the back seat. As Miles got in the front, Ingrid introduced Belinda Mae Cerrone, sitting to her right. "She's a dancer," Ingrid said. "We're in dance class together on the base."

"Ingrid's the best," Belinda Mae said in a high nasal voice, edged enough to trouble the ear. "She's better than the teachers."

"Belinda was a chorus girl on Broadway before she got married," Ingrid said.

"I tried out for the Rockettes, but they chose someone taller."

"*You* did ballet, didn't you?" Miles asked Ingrid.

"Ballet and modern dance. Tap, too. Sometimes I wish I'd done shows. Belinda Mae was in *Goldilocks*."

"It closed too soon," Belinda Mae said sadly.

"Who did the choreography?" Ingrid asked Belinda Mae.

"Agnes de Mille," Belinda Mae said. "Do you know her?"

"I met her twice when I was in New York."

"That's really cool," Belinda Mae said.

"What's your husband do?" Oliver asked Belinda Mae over his shoulder. The Jaguar drifted to the edge of the narrow road. Oliver jerk-corrected the car back on the road.

"Be careful!" Ingrid admonished. Miles frowned with concern; it had been too close for comfort.

"He does maintenance," Belinda Mae said to answer Oliver's question. "He's an engineer. We have two children. Three and one."

Talk lagged for many seconds as everyone recovered from the near accident.

Finally, Ingrid said, "Belinda and I will be dancing in the base Christmas-show this year."

"Yeah," Belinda Mae said.

"Save me a ticket," Miles said.

"It's free," Belinda Mae said unnecessarily.

They dined at Le Cheverny restaurant in Limoges and drove about twelve miles northwest to Oradour-Sur-Glane. Over coffee after lunch, Ingrid talked about what she'd learned as a base-approved tour guide.

"I've never heard of Oradour," Miles said.

"It's not well known to Americans. People don't want to think about it."

"About what?" Belinda Mae said.

"German atrocities."

"This was where they took place?" Belinda Mae asked with uninformed astonishment. "When was it?"

"During the occupation," Ingrid said.

"Who did it?"

"The SS," Oliver said.

"What's that?" Belinda Mae asked.

"The Fuhrer's security guard. They had unlimited authority."

"A license to murder innocents," Miles added.

"They annihilated everyone and everything," Oliver said.

"Wow," Belinda Mae said vaguely.

Ingrid felt Belinda Mae's response disrespectful. "Six hundred and forty-two villagers were massacred on June 10, 1944, four days after the D-Day invasion, by more than two hundred German soldiers of the Second SS Panzer Division."

"The whole town?" Belinda Mae said, agonized by the truth.

"Seven people survived," Ingrid said, bearing grief for innocents killed without justice, or a trial, or any wrongdoing in the first place.

"It's hard to imagine," Miles said.

The group went silent.

They finished lunch and drove to the town.

The four seldom spoke as they walked up to town center. Nothing had changed in eighteen years. Skeleton forms of buildings surrounded by rubble mixed among contrasting vibrant scrubs and healthy green grass. Rusting shells of burned; tireless vehicles were scattered on streets and yards. A metal bed frame lay twisted and distorted from fire. A rusted stove. A sewing machine seemed to teeter on the ledge of the partial remains of a window. Metal utensils, automobile tire rims, bicycle frames. A restrained miasma bore the onus of innocent lives extinguished.

"I never can fathom that amount of hate and evil," Ingrid said.

"They would say they were just following orders," Oliver said.

"Still, what about them as individuals allowed them to kill innocent women and children?" Ingrid asked. She stopped and looked at a map. She pointed to charred ruins near the town edge. "The men were forced into barns and burned to death."

"Why didn't they run?" Belinda Mae asked.

"Many were shot in the legs so they couldn't escape."

"They should have fought back," Belinda Mae said.

"They were villagers, Belinda Mae," Ingrid said. "Farmers. Not soldiers."

"Were they after Jews?" Oliver asked.

"I don't think they specifically targeted Jews on this day," Ingrid said. "There were seven Jewish refugees among those killed, but I think this was more to intimidate the Resistance."

As they walked, they passed a painted metal sign on the ground near the door of a store—BOULANGERIE, the painted letters scored and marred. Inside, between ruined walls, an oven door hung down, dented and tilted to one side, attached by only one hinge.

They came to the church. "This is where the women and children were imprisoned behind locked doors," Ingrid said.

"Children?" Belinda Mae moaned.

"More than two hundred."

They entered the interior of what remained.

"How could they do this?" Miles asked.

"It is incomprehensible," Ingrid replied.

Inside the church, the exterior walls were partially intact but crumbling. Much of the roof was destroyed and indirect early-afternoon sun filtered diffused light to throw ragged-edged shadows on the dirt floor and decrepit walls. In the center of the sanctuary, the skeletal metal-remains of a pram lay flattened on the dirt floor.

Behind the remains of the altar at the back of the church, Ingrid pointed up to arched window frames now without their original stained glass or lead frameworks.

"One woman escaped through there and lived," Ingrid said, pointing to where the central had been. "She found a ladder used for lighting candles and climbed to that window—with a full-size standing image of Christ—and broke the stained glass. As she thrust herself out, a machine gunner landed four shots in her body. Half-conscious, she fell twelve feet to the ground."

At the far edge of town, they began to retrace their steps back to the car.

"Was anyone ever punished?" Miles asked Ingrid.

"Some have been tried and convicted. But most of the sentences were reversed or not enforced. Others acquitted."

For a few minutes, all four remained quiet, consumed by their private thoughts.

"It's hard for me to process what happened," Miles said as they were under way on their return to base. "It was so definitive and irrevocable."

"I try not to imagine it," Ingrid said. "The cruelty. We need to pray for the victims and move on."

"Lot of good praying will do," Oliver said.

There can't be any harm in it, Miles thought.

"Never forget," Ingrid said. "I'm going to write about it. There are so many stories that must be told."

A somber mood prevailed.

They returned to the base in just under an hour and took Belinda Mae to her quarters. On the return to Brassioux, Oliver turned to Ingrid. "Why did you ask that Belinda Mae person?"

"She's alone, Ollie. Her husband works on C-130s all the time. She's sweet and lonely."

"Her brain is molasses," Oliver said.

"That's not fair. She's kind, sensitive, and a loving mother. In many ways, a special human being."

"A waste of time," he said.

Ingrid's breathing quickened with the disagreement. Miles remained silent. Minutes later, when they reached Brassioux, the persistent ill feeling between Oliver and Ingrid made Miles uneasy, and he was sorry. He liked them both.

***

Ingrid had read many articles on the Holocaust by a professor at the *École normale supérieure*, Dennis Martin. He was an obvious essential resource for her book. Miles's French teacher's brother had known the professor in school, and he arranged an appointment for Ingrid. Ingrid asked Alyce, as a journalist, if she would like to come along, and they traveled to Paris for a visit. The professor greeted them in his small second-floor office.

Ingrid and Alyce took their seats in two wooden armless chairs facing the professor, who sat behind a kneehole mahogany writing desk, its tooled leather top clear except for a pen inkstand, and an open appointment book. The professor had unkempt dark hair streaked with strands of gray, and he peered at them with watery, dark-brown eyes over half-circle reading glasses in wire frames.

"What is your book about?" the professor asked Ingrid.

"I've started to write about my family members during the Occupation. I'm looking for insights into their ordeal. And where I can learn more."

"You must know I lived through those times," the professor said.

"Yes. From your writings."

"And you, Mademoiselle?" he asked Alyce. "What may I do for you?"

"I'm a writer for the *International Herald Tribune*. I'm writing documentary articles on events and people. The more I learn about the Holocaust, the more difficult I find it is to verify facts," Alyce said.

"Or find facts at all," said Ingrid.

The professor nodded. "Part of that is the revision of history by the deniers who falsely profess that the Holocaust never happened, that it's a hoax perpetrated by the Jews. The Nazis were terribly effective in keeping the genocide in the camps hidden. And then, during the liberation, they systematically destroyed documents and evidence.

"How many were killed?" Alyce asked.

"Millions. We'll never know a reasonable estimate. But it was extensive. They developed a brutal and effective system for killing. The crematoria at Auschwitz-Birkenau could incinerate up to six thousand corpses a day."

"Was genocide just to elevate Aryans to world domination?" Ingrid asked.

"European domination at least. It certainly played a major role," the professor said. "The Nazis wanted a society of alikes and despised those nonconformists to the Aryan image."

"Aryan, meaning . . . ?"

"Caucasian and not of Jewish descent. But the designation became blurred. By Nazi definition, a Gypsy would be Aryan. The Gypsy population had increased in Europe for centuries, and the Nazis needed to classify them as non-Aryan so as to include them in the deadly cleansing. So the Nazis altered the Nuremberg Laws. They deprived Jews of German citizenship, designating them "subjects of the state" and limiting business, preventing intermarriages, performing sterilization. The Gypsies were added to the law as nonconformists. They became nonpersons, people of 'foreign blood' and 'labor-shy,' part of the 'asocials.' Under Hitler's authority, Himmler began the extermination of the Gypsies—more than twenty thousand at Auschwitz alone."

"When did the killing start?" Alyce asked.

"In September 1939, a secret program known as euthanasia began the systematic murder of German, Austrian, and Polish hospital patients with mental or physical disabilities. By 1941, massacres of Jews and non-Jew undesirables were accomplished by gassing, shooting, hanging."

"People are forgetting the horrors, professor," Ingrid said. "Are you concerned it could happen again?"

"It's a fundamental question. I believe, without doubt, it will happen again in some form. Massacres have been in societies for millennia."

"What have we learned?" Ingrid asked, reaching into her handbag for her copy of Nietzsche's nineteenth-century writings and her notebook. "The concept of a superior master race has been discussed in German academia for a long time. Nietzsche thinks about the master race and slaves."

"The intelligentsia of the nineteenth century accepted the premise of superiority," the professor said. "Have you read Hitler's autobiography, *Mein Kampf*? Nietzsche greatly influenced it."

"I've tried to find a copy."

"It's against the law to publish or distribute it in some countries."

"I tried in the States. It wasn't available in libraries or bookstores."

The professor rose to retrieve a book from the shelves behind him. "I bought this early second edition that the Nazi government distributed to be read by soldiers and civil servants. It contains both volumes. I'll loan it to you, but I need it back within two weeks. I reference it often."

Ingrid accepted and expressed her gratitude. She glanced at Alyce to let her know she would share. Alyce had her diary open in her lap. She wrote notes.

"What are the signs, professor?" Alyce asked. "What alerts us to the danger?"

"I have come to believe genocide is consequence of change in the composition of society and culture. A change in belief and perception and core values of a social group. If there is a hereditary factor, it is minor."

"Really? In Germany, fathers, sons, even mothers participated in the killing. Doesn't that reflect a hereditary factor of the willingness or the desire to kill innocents?"

"Of course, I don't know," the professor said. "But it's not wise to think genetics is the major influence in an individual's contribution to a massacre. I believe an individual ability to kill innocents is an aberration of the involved individual's free will and morality. We're all products of our genetic inheritance, but to participate in massacre is the emergence in society of vicious beliefs that killing others for racial or nonconformist cleansing is justified. I believe individuals have responsibility to not succumb to such evil."

"Does absence of religion play a role?" Alyce asked.

"I don't know. Certainly, the aberration of morality would play a role. But genocide is not justified by belief that victims are consigned to an afterlife for their benefit. The Germans made that argument when they called the killing of mentally or physically disabled hospitalized patients—it was called 'euthanasia'—when their purpose clearly was to cleanse human existence of what they saw as undesirables. Do you see?"

Ingrid and Alyce nodded.

"It's hard to know individual motives in the aftermath," Alyce said, "and it's after the fact. Are the changes in society that might suggest justification for mass murders?"

"In our times, democratic governance with free speech and fairly elected politicians who govern by consensus of a majority seem to make the emergence of massacres less likely. So a major societal change by autocratic leaders who seek absolute power is a threat. These leaders will dismantle democratic societies. They'll remove adversaries from office and physically and mentally incapacitating them by poisoning or assassination. They disrupt elections so the majority's will is not known. And the autocrats are consummate liars, bringing fear of an uncertain future or a false perception of danger of nonconformists to a populace to motivate them to hostile action. And the autocrat uses myths to incite crowds. Hitler was a master of this. He used anti-Semitic canards and the myth of blood libel to inflame hate in his followers.

"I don't know what blood libel is," Alyce said.

Ingrid answered. "It's the false inflammatory characterization that Jews murder Christian children or gentiles to use their blood in the performance of religious rituals for healing—false accusations that reach back to the birth of Christianity. It has been a major theme in the persecution of Jews for centuries."

"Exactly," said the professor. "And Hitler used many false claims of Jews being responsible for promoting the rise of communism, or they were collectively responsible for the persecution of Jesus. These anti-Semitic canards were central to Hitler's worldview, and they've persisted for millennia and into the present. To find out more, here is the name of an Oradure survivor who speaks out about the tragedy. He lives in Tours now." He wrote a name and address on a scrap of paper. "Also, you might investigate details of Dachau. It was the first camp established. Early on, it housed Russian prisoners, intellectuals, and political adversaries; only later did incarcerations of Jews and women become common as gas chambers and crematoria were constructed. These were not destroyed at Dachau. I have the name of a Jewish survivor who is documenting and identifying Dachau victims. He also has pictures from the Americans of the horrors discovered at liberation. So much of the remaining evidence is classified. And he is an historian documenting Jewish incarceration in Drance, here in Paris. It was a transit facility where tens of thousands of Jews were arrested by French police to be transferred to Auschwitz. You might find details about relatives."

Alyce and Ingrid thanked the professor warmly for his time and for sharing his knowledge. He was a special person, and Ingrid felt inadequate to express the measure of her appreciation.

Within two weeks, Ingrid and Alyce flew to Munich and borrowed a car to visit Dachau. Emile Bloom was in his seventies, slight and withered, but with a bright countenance.

"You were in the French Resistance?" Alyce asked.

"I was, yes."

"Yet you live here?"

"For only the last three years, as part of my research."

"You lived in Châteauroux?"

"Near Limoges. I came to Germany after my wife died. My son is in America, and my daughter married a Swiss shop owner."

"I've brought a list of family names," Ingrid said.

"Come into the back room."

They went into what had been a bedroom. A small table served as a desk with a straight-backed, armless, factory-made chair. There was no place for Ingrid or Alyce to sit.

The man opened the top drawer of a chest-high, four-drawer filing cabinet. "Read me your names one by one."

With each name he searched three or four places in different drawers. Twenty minutes later, he opened a folder from the middle drawer. "Abraham Sternberg," he said. "Arrested as a Jew, a professor at university. Was he French?" he asked Ingrid.

"I do think he's family. I think he was Polish, on my husband's father's side."

"Incarcerated, April 1942. Died of typhus, November 12, 1944. Does that seem right? It's a common name," Emile said, showing her the entry.

"Do you see others?"

"This is the only one. But I think it's one of the ones you're looking for."

"Can you tell me how it would have been for him?"

"Are you visiting today?"

"Yes."

"May I go with you? I can show you what I've learned. It's only recently has Dachau been open to the public for limited access. The camp has been under American control since liberation and changed little in these eighteen years. It's my mission to have people sense what victims felt and endured."

"That would be very helpful, *monsieur*," Ingrid said.

"Are records accessible?" Alyce asked.

"Many were destroyed as the liberators approached. Those that exist are not easily accessed. Official channels are useless. Material is often classified."

"By the Americans? Why?"

"There is photographic evidence of American soldiers executing prison guards on the day of liberation. And later, too."

"How do I find evidence?" Alyce asked.

"With my fellow documentarians, we bribe, coerce, finagle, plead. Much of our information comes from talking with survivors. It takes time."

"It's so horrible. You have my deepest sympathy," Alyce said.

"Thank you, *mademoiselle*. But, of course, I tell you for the opportunity to tell the world what happened. So many Germans and collaborators deny the camps ever existed. Others claim they were exclusively for incarceration of political activists. So much is unknown."

They parked outside the Dachau camp.

"It's not uncommon for local citizens to refuse to answer when asked by visitors where they can find the camp," Emile said. "Many declare no knowledge of the camp or its purpose. But the liberators were so appalled by the tolerance of the Dachau citizens to what they found in the camp, they forced them to bury thousands of the murdered."

As they approached an entrance gate, Emile pointed to the words forged in iron. "*Arbeit macht frei*," Emile said in German. "Work makes one free. The camp opened in 1933. At first, prisoners were brought to work to build the camp, but then to work in private industry, and as the war expanded, forced to work in armament plants. Look. You can see the barracks."

He directed them to move beyond an obstruction. "Thirty-two barracks were built to house two hundred to two hundred and fifty occupants each. At the time of liberation, each barrack contained sixteen hundred to two thousand prisoners."

They walked toward the crematorium section. "Is that what I think it is?" Alyce asked. She pointed to an eight-yard-long, waist-high mound of packed gray soot, solidified over time.

"Human ashes," Emile confirmed.

As they entered what looked like a building for showers, Emile said that it was where euthanasia was conducted. "It's amazing how the truth is obscured about these rooms. I've found photographs of prisoners in here, waiting to be disrobed for lice cleansing. Then gassed. And let me show what I've learned from objective visitors. Look at that sign," he said. "BRAUSEBAD. That means 'shower bath.' That seems defensive irony to me. Especially when there is no evidence of water pipes or showerheads."

They walked through the rooms. "Those vents were where the gas was introduced," Emile said. Vents on the walls and floors were obvious. Emile led them outside into the hall and pointed to a metal blower and small box. "This is undoubtedly where the cyanide pellets were vaporized. They're connected to the vents into the room."

"How can anyone doubt the evidence?" Ingrid wondered.

"It has been repeatedly reported the prisoners were euthanized at another facility, denying the killings at Dachau. Typical of the confused distortion of the truth associated with this and other camps."

They went into the crematorium. Two brick ovens, still covered with dark deposits, were positioned side by side.

"I have seen a photograph taken on the day after liberation where two survivors placed a corpse on a plank on track rollers to demonstrate the head-first insertion."

"Were they burned alive?" Ingrid asked, her voice quavering.

"I don't believe so. As death from starvation and diseases became rampant, and tens of thousands executed, the dead were cremated here."

Alyce took pictures.

Before they left, Emile took them to a single railroad track with thirty railroad cars, many doors still open. On arrival, each of the cars had been packed with decomposing corpses of prisoners mixed with the near-dead.

And as they continued over the grounds, Emile said, "More than thirty-six hundred unburied, many naked, corpses in grotesque thrashes of death, some disembodied, were clumped into piles near the train. Near this area, on a camp dirt path, others lay alone in tortured, indignant positions on paths as if they were trying to crawl to freedom. I've seen classified photographs."

"Were the guards punished?"

"There is no doubt, some American soldiers executed guards. Some say no more than fifty. Others believe up to a thousand guards were killed. The truth will never be known."

Ingrid, grieved by the extent of her distress, said to Alyce, "It's time to go, don't you think?"

Alyce nodded.

They thanked Emile, exchanged addresses, and returned to the airport.

PART TWO
1962–63

CHAPTER 8
Skiing the Tyrol

February 1962

The wonder and excitement of skiing in the Austrian Tyrol was a yearly diversion for many personnel on base at Châteauroux and, as a top tour guide for personnel, Ingrid arranged a trip to include doctors and other staff from the hospital. Oliver, who had skied in Colorado, George and Anne Pingree from northern Utah, and Angus Peabody from Bangor, Maine, were expert skiers; Miles, Ingrid, Carl Brooks from Texas, and Tamara, Angus's wife, were inexperienced and spent two days training and learning on bunny slopes at the resort before taking to the steeper slopes with their instructors.

They started from the base in a private hired van leased by the US government for nonofficial excursions. After a few minutes on the road, Ingrid stood, taking the guide's microphone at the front of the bus to speak to all the passengers.

"Welcome! This tour is organized by base travel and recreation department. Many of you don't know our doctors at the hospital, and since we'll be together for almost a week, I'd like you to make their acquaintance."

She called on Texan Carl Brooks to speak to the group, a GMO. He was shy and reserved and likely unknown to most and to a few others only in passing. "Tell us about yourself, Carl." Carl came forward as Ingrid returned to her seat next to Oliver and stood in the aisle at the front of the van.

"Hello to all those I don't know. And good to see my colleagues. My name is Carl Brooks, here from Abilene, Texas. Since there are no ski resorts in Texas, I'm not looking to impress folks on the slopes. So, I hope you'll remember, I'm a companion and worthy of an ounce of pity when I fall." He smiled.

"What should we call you, Doc?" someone called out from the back.

"We're off base now. Call me Carl."

Ingrid turned to the passengers. "And I'm Ingrid. We're all on a first-name basis."

Carl continued, "Well, I grew up in Abilene and went to Texas Tech, and I knew folks from Dyess Air Force base. They were good people. And after med school I wanted to join the Air Force."

"Carl's in for life," Angus called out.

"Not quite. Twenty at most," Carl said. He continued, "I got drafted after an internship in Austin and just signed on thinking it was the best career I could have."

"You married, Carl?" Angus baited.

"Heavens to Betsy, no. Never found a girl who thought I was good enough."

"Maybe on this trip, some Fräulein will take a fancy to you," Angus continued. "Right?"

"Well, I thank you for that, Doctor. Certainly do appreciate the thought."

"What do you do outside the hospital?" Ingrid asked. "Haven't I seen some of your work in the commissary gift shop?"

"Yep. I do them painted wood carvings of a cowpoke, the ones with him holdin' onto a calf in front of the saddle with its belly down and legs dangling down each side of the horse. I named it Almost Home."

"I've seen those," Anne Pingree said. "They're beautiful, Carl."

"Thank you, ma'am."

"Can't hear from back here," someone said.

"Speak louder," Ingrid whispered to Carl.

"So, you ride?" Ingrid asked so all could hear.

"Worked a ranch in north Texas for a couple years."

"Where'd you learn to carve?"

"My granddaddy."

"Well, we need to find you a companion on this trip," Angus's wife said. "You deserve a good friend."

Carl dropped his head, his forehead wrinkled, cheeks flushed behind two-day growth of 'off-duty' beard. "Now I don't want you thinking that. I signed on for skiing."

Ingrid leaned over to Oliver. "Tell them about us," she said.

"Jesus," Oliver said, "not one of my talents."

She lowered her voice. "Just do it. We need to make this a compatible group."

Oliver stood and took the microphone as Carl sat down.

"I met Ingrid when we were in high school together in New York. Then we went to separate colleges, Ingrid went to Finch College in Manhattan and I went to UMass. I've skied in Colorado and Utah mostly. She's a beginner."

Ingrid turned to Angus and Tamara. Angus took the microphone and spoke loudly over the engine's fluctuating drone. He told of his family heritage as lobsterman on the Maine coast. He and Tamara had married when they were young and had four children.

"I've never tried to ski," Tamara added.

"She's not athletic," Angus said.

"I am too!" Tamara rebuked. "I played field hockey in high school."

"That doesn't count," Angus said, speaking tersely to Tamara.

"That poor woman," Ingrid whispered to Oliver through clenched teeth without turning her head.

"Can't hear back here," someone said again.

After Angus sat down, a few others introduced themselves, and in the silence that followed, Ingrid got up and asked the driver about their arrival time. He replied in French, but she understood.

"There is a rest stop ahead," she announced. "Then it will be about two more hours to the border; we'll arrive around five."

She visually surveyed the passengers. She was pleased; most seemed satisfied and eager to arrive.

***

On the sixth day of the trip, before their scheduled departure, they all had an early breakfast before daylight in the lodge. Clouds layered close to the earth, scraping the peaks of the mountains and dropping heavy snowflakes on an already dense snowpack. Oliver, George and Anne Pingree, and Angus, as the expert skiers, took the first cable car out to the highest run. The beginners—Miles, Ingrid, Carl, and Tamara—relaxed for an hour or so before taking a half-empty, eight-passenger gondola to a lesser peak.

"Have you enjoyed yourselves so far?" Ingrid asked Carl and Tamara.

"The best," Carl said.

"I've worried about the children," Tamara said, "and yesterday was hard work."

"But you've done really well," Ingrid said. "You're amazingly agile."

"Learning to ski made me focus, keep my mind off the base," Tamara said. "It was relaxing."

"You've really improved," Miles told her.

Tamara smiled. She had always believed she could ski, and Miles's words pleased her. She wished Angus had said them.

The front of the cab angled with forward motion as metal cables lifted it with slow, jerky momentum from the station to the first steel tower. They looked out the windows on all four sides of the gondola. After fifteen minutes into the twenty-minute ride, the terrible rumble of a landslide deafened the skiers. Thousands of tons of snow cascaded down the mountain from above. A rolling wave of the advancing edge threw sheets of snow and mist into the air.

"It's going to hit us," Carl yelled again.

"Get down on the floor," Miles cried. He and Ingrid were still face down, but Carl and Tamara froze, still standing, clutching metal poles that extended from floor to ceiling.

The gondola was still moving, and the tower they'd just passed cracked as if made of toothpicks and fell over, steel cables snapping like gunshots.

And then a deafening crack as the support cable snapped and an instant screech of cable on cable.

Dead silence surrounded them; the cab swayed on the swinging cables.

A second wave of snow continued the onslaught.

"It's going to hit us," Carl yelled again.

Miles and Ingrid were face down holding on to a metal bench support and Carl and Tamara were upright clinging desperately to the support poles. "Get down on the floor," Miles cried out again.

The gondola lurched.

"My god," Carl screamed.

Tamara moaned.

A loud crack and another roar from the second mass of the avalanche passed below them; it engulfed the cable-support column and the cab lurched violently as a cable clanged against metal. Carl and Tamara were hurled to the foot of the pitched cab. Miles and Ingrid, still on the floor, clung to the oscillating central pole.

"Everyone all right?" Miles shouted.

Then the last intact support cable gave an ear-piercing snap, the gondola plunged one hundred feet straight down entering the snow end-first, throwing Ingrid and Miles down onto the forms of Carl and Tamara. The upper half of the cab was enshrouded by pulsing currents of swirling snow. Miles touched Ingrid. No response.

"Carl!" he called out. Then "Tamara!"

But there was no response. The two of them were lying face-up at the lowest end of the cab. Miles immediately turned Ingrid over. She was breathing. He unbuttoned her coat and felt the quickened pulse in her neck artery. Miles crawled to the corner where Carl lay only a few feet away. The swirling snow around the exposed part of the cab had settled and there was enough light to see Carl's head twisted and bent back at close to a right angle. Miles removed a ski glove but could find no pulse. He positioned his ear close to Carl's gaping mouth but there was no breath, his neck fractured at the cervical spine.

Miles slid to where Tamara lay on her back, her face bruised and bleeding, arms splayed. A metal strip from a window casing had pene-trated her coat, entering her abdomen just below the sternum. Blood darkened her coat where the metal strip had entered, and with the six inches still exposed, it pulsed with the beat of her failing heart. Her eyes were open. She coughed and gagged, blood spewing from her mouth. Miles unbuttoned the coat from the bottom, careful not to disturb the strip—movement or removal would only increase the hemorrhage. Miles ripped the dress near the wound; there was an eight-inch laceration with fat oozing over the edges next to the entrance wound. The bleeding in the abdomen bloated the stomach, pressing on the rib cage and crushing the lungs, reducing her air intake to faint, useless gasps. Below Tamara's chin, a gushing stream of blood obscured the Velcro fastener. He ripped open the torn sweatshirt parka from the bottom. Tamara cried out, a harsh sound without meaning. Her form went flaccid, her eyes fixed on Miles, the hardened fear of her look dissipated just before her eyelids half closed, and she died.

Miles moved closer to Ingrid still lying on the floor, motionless, her face void of any conscious movement. Her pulse was strong in the eighties, her breathing was shallow at twenty. He positioned her head to keep the airway clear. He found reflexes in her extremities. She had swelling on the back of her head, her pupils half dilated but equal and both contracted; his shadow shifted and the faint light from the exposed front of the cab illuminated her eyes. Frost began to accumulate on her disheveled hair. Her hands were cold; he put the one glove that had fallen off back on. She had a concussion, which he could not treat there. He would keep her as warm as he could and hope she regained consciousness. He lay beside her, his arms around her from the back, her head cradled on his right arm so together they mutually conserved heat.

She moaned and half opened her eyes.

"Can you hear me?" Miles asked.

She nodded ever so slightly.

"We're going to make it," he said.

"The others," she whispered.

"Resolved."

She closed her eyes. He held her firmly for many minutes until her eyes half opened again.

He leaned close to her. "Hang in there. Don't ever give up." *You're the best.*

With the greatest effort, she opened her eyes and looked to the side to see him. The corners of her mouth tipped up slightly in the best smile she could muster.

"I'm here," he said.

Her smile widened, and she tried to speak but a sound came out like the cry of a baby kitten.

"Don't leave me," he said.

She nodded just before she lost consciousness.

After another hour, he lost awareness of time but resisted with reciting poems and passages he could remember and doing division math to prevent the peril of unconsciousness and to be sure Ingrid's breathing remained unobstructed.

Three hours later, she moved, her head turning, her arm reaching out briefly before falling limp again.

Twelve hours later, it was dark. Now in a semiconscious fog, he heard the clatter of an approaching snow cat. He sat up, still holding Ingrid. When the yellow cone of a torch swept over the interior, he gripped her tighter. He could feel she was alive. The noise of a crowbar straining, then pounding to clear an opening by breaking the window and cutting through steel caused Ingrid to shudder, then relax. Her eyelids quivered but were still closed. The scraping and pounding continued.

"Do you hurt?" Miles said leaning close so his lips touched her ear.

She moaned, "Where are we?"

"On the mountain," Miles said.

"Will we die?"

He held her more firmly so she could sense he was with her.

"Rescue is here," he said.

She moaned a sigh, drifting into unconsciousness again.

He feared for a world without Ingrid and wondered why he had never fully realized the value of her companionship until now.

Both were taken to the hospital. Ingrid had a concussion but no signs of brain damage or internal cranial bleeding. She was in intensive care for constant observation, awake, but disoriented and sedated. Miles was admitted for hydration and observation. Oliver, George, Ann, and Angus were on a more difficult mountain that was untouched by the disaster.

Oliver came to see Miles after he had checked on Ingrid. She was going to be all right. He said the remains of Carl and Tamara had been transferred to Innsbruck and were ready for return to Châteauroux.

"Thanks," Oliver said to Miles. "You saved her life."

"Are they sure she's, okay?"

"Everyone is confident she'll recover."

"I haven't seen a doc yet," Miles said.

"A neurosurgeon saw you when you were sedated. They'll keep you in hospital for another day or so, then I'll hire a van to take you and the others back."

"And Ingrid?"

"She'll soon be out of intensive care, but they'll observe her for a few more days. I'll be with her and bring her home when it's time."

"I think I'll give up skiing," Miles said.

"I'm with you, my man. Never again."

CHAPTER 9
Bruce and Ina

1962
Miles

Miles had encountered Master Sergeant Bruce McKenzie and his wife, Ina, who lived across the street and down a few houses, on their walks around Brassioux and had spent many minutes in pleasant stand-up conversations. One evening, they invited him to a homecooked dinner. Bring a guest, they said. Night after next.

Miles asked Oliver who declined because he was on in-house hospital call.

"But be careful socializing with NCOs," Oliver said emphatically.

"He's a genuine human being," Miles said.

"Hey, you're a commissioned officer with responsibilities of no socialization with those of lower rank. It weakens discipline. That's Springer's rule."

"There's no harm," Miles said.

"Well, I can't go," Oliver said. "Ask Ingrid if you want."

Ingrid knew of the McKenzies and was pleased to attend.

Ina had set a table for four with a white linen tablecloth, sterling silver utensils, Limoges china, and Waterford crystal, all procured through weekend excursions to ever-prevalent antique shops in France.

During dinner Ingrid commented on the paintings on the walls they'd seen.

"Bruce does them," Ina said.

"They're so accomplished."

"Is there one you especially like?" Bruce asked.

"They're all pleasing," Ingrid said. "I especially like that one of the road lined with Italian poplars over the sideboard."

"How did you learn to do this?" Miles asked Bruce.

"I painted for years without satisfaction at home, but when I got here, I had the time to study with Gertrude Fineman. She had a studio near Arles. Have you heard of her?"

Neither Ingrid nor Miles knew of her.

"Do either of you paint?" Bruce asked.

"Not even barns," Miles said.

"I do paint, and I love to draw caricatures in ink," Ingrid said. "I've studied art for years but without much artistic accomplishment. It's hard to find a good teacher."

"Gertrude was cantankerous and eccentric, but she excelled at teaching," Bruce said. "She survived incarceration as a Jew in Bergen-Belsen and died four years ago from cancer. I value every minute I was able to spend with her. Ina and Gertrude collaborated in some fantastic meals for village friends in Arles."

"You teach here on base?" Ingrid asked.

"He teaches in our spare room," Ina said.

"It's what I want to do when I get out," Bruce said. "Retire from the military and teach art."

"What medium?" Ingrid asked.

"Primarily oil on canvas. I study famous artists of the past; it helps me improve my craft and create ideas. Paris is unique for learning great techniques of the past."

"How does an artist become uniquely individual?" Ingrid asked. "Everything seems to have been done."

"I'm not sure that's true," Bruce said. "Every human brings their own perspective on the world, and they make a unique contribution, even if it's imitative in some way."

"But how can we stand out?"

"Determine what beauty is to you, and create it in your art."

"That sounds impossible," Ingrid smiled.

Ina laughed affection for her husband. "Careful, Ingrid. You've triggered Bruce's lecture."

"I'd love it," Ingrid said.

"Non-artists' views of art are so different," Bruce began. "You go to the Louvre, there are patrons who glance and pause for a fraction of a minute at a famous painting. They feel self-important, believing just looking at a famous work makes them more erudite. But there are others who spend hours engaged in a work of art that gives them pleasure. It evokes an emotion and seems to bind them to the artist's passion for creating. The work gives meaning about the subject matter—and the artist."

Ingrid's candid interest and her admiration for Bruce's knowledge occupied Miles's attention more than Bruce's specific thoughts. Ingrid's caring for others seemed unique and genuine, and totally unaffected.

"Isn't value a factor of a patron's attention and respect?" Ingrid asked. "Interest in the highest price paid?"

"Yes. Exactly," Bruce said. "But those 'investor patrons' often miss the opportunity to enrich their lives through art."

"How can I learn more?" Ingrid said.

Bruce looked at Ina and raised his eyebrows, silently asking her opinion.

Ina nodded and began clearing the table. "I'll limit him to ten minutes at the most," Ina said, "then we'll have a glass of aged Coteaux du Layon with cheese."

Bruce went into the back of the house and returned with a portfolio of papers. He laid five pieces of paper, all approximately the same size, in a stack on the table in front of Ingrid—a circle, a triangle, a square, a parallelogram, and a five-pointed star:

"Use all the shapes and place them together in a way that pleases you," Bruce said.

"Any rules?" Ingrid asked.

"They all have to be touching."

Ingrid positioned the shapes with the edges touching.

She looked to Bruce for comment. "Are you pleased?" he asked her.

"I don't know that I'm pleased," Ingrid said. "But I did line them up all touching."

"Miles, come look. What's your reaction? Does it interest you? Does the positioning make you want to continue to look?"

"The truth?"

"Please."

"Not at all."

Bruce reached over and changed the positions of the shapes.

"What do you think now, Miles?" Bruce asked.

"That's not fair," Ingrid said. "You didn't say I could lay them on top of one another."

"Isn't that touching?" he said to Ingrid, then to Miles, "Comparing the two arrangements, which do you prefer now?"

"The last one," Miles said, pointing to new positions of the star and the circle.

"What's that got to do with making my art better?" Ingrid asked, feeling slighted at being second best to Miles's judgment.

"We ask ourselves what is beautiful for us. That's different for each of us. If we can define elements of beauty that please us, make us enjoy, stimulate our memory, we begin to incorporate that self-aware knowledge into our art."

Ingrid shook her head. "I hear you, but I can't process the idea of what you showed me."

"Look there," Bruce said to both Ingrid and Miles pointing to the painting over the sideboard of a road lined with poplar trees. You said that pleased you. What did you find about the painting that made you say that?"

"I like the scene," Ingrid said.

"So it's the choice of content that you like. The French countryside."

"I think so."

"I tried to reproduce the scene as I saw it. Representational art. An imitation of what actually exists."

"I think you captured the beauty of the moment," Ingrid said.

"Thank you. But in an imitative way, not imaginative. Think of van Gogh. Whether you like his work or not, it's memorable, creative, unique. And it moves people. Think of *Starry Night*, or *Bedroom in Arles*. He *created* art. He made his work felt by others."

"How would you wish you had done your scene over the sideboard?" Ingrid asked.

"Think for a moment in shapes. I wish the 'road' slab was more two-dimensional, the sides closer to parallel. And I wish there had been some variance in the rendering, a suggestion of a curve, maybe, or a straight object like a tree at an angle fallen over the road. I should have experimented with brushstrokes, found something less meticulous and less stringent. I should have made the line of trees off-center. It's helpful to practice construction of a scene as shapes and colors that you've chosen for elements that are pleasing to you as the structure of your final work."

"But how do you know what is beautiful for our viewers?"

"We don't for all viewers, of course. 'Beauty is in the eye of the beholder.' But if we're good at our craft, our art moves many viewers in some way, evokes emotion or understanding of a thought or feeling. Through art, the artist transmits a passion, a love, respect, an intensity, even anger or condemnation that moves the viewer. Of course, as artists, we're never successful for all viewers."

"So how does that relate to me if I wanted to create a painting?" Miles asked. "Would I just do what Picasso did?"

"And Braque? The originators of Cubism?" Bruce said. "You could, but to copy them limits the boundaries of your creative imagination. I think we are inspired by others, but we must not be copiers. It's best to seek elements of another's success and use them to discover your originality."

"How do you do that?"

"Gertrude had me spend weeks in the Louvre sketching and painting, discovering ideas in the works of others. I learned elements of painting pictures that taught me principles I would use uniquely in my own art."

"Doesn't art have to look familiar in some way?" Miles asked.

"Not at all. There can be art for some with an intersection of two thin black lines."

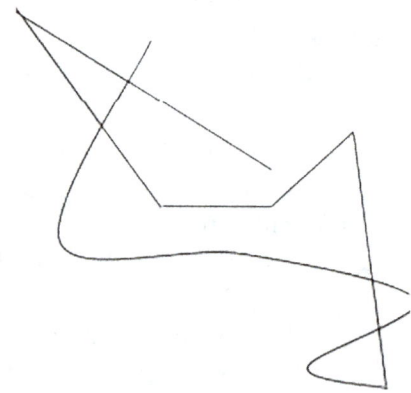

"There are so many characteristics that might move you. It could be color appropriation. Differences in dimensions, shape positions, hues."

Ina approached with a tray of cheese, a plate of fresh-baked macarons, and four glasses of wine. "That's a good place to break," Ina said.

As Miles walked with Ingrid back to her house, both were silent for more than a minute.

"Thanks for taking me," Ingrid said. "What extraordinary people."

"Bruce taught me a lot in a short time," Miles said.

"I wish I could learn from him," Ingrid said.

"When you were in the 'ladies', I asked him if he would take me on as a student. He said he'd work it out."

"I was thinking about that too. I just didn't know how to ask him."

Miles stopped. "We'll go back," he said.

"Really?"

"Why not give it a try?"

Ingrid smiled.

A few minutes later they were at the house. Bruce opened the front door. Ina was in the kitchen. "What's up?" he asked.

"Ingrid wants to take lessons," Miles said.

"Could I?" Ingrid asked.

Bruce thought for a few seconds. "The problem is I'm only going to have the one evening open on the schedule. A Thursday."

"Could we alternate every other week then?" Miles asked.

"Better yet, could we come together *every* week?" Ingrid asked.

"Do you have room?" Miles asked, liking Ingrid's idea.

Bruce concentrated for a few seconds. "I could make room for you guys," he said, smiling. "I'm sure you two would be my best students."

"Can we start next week?" Miles asked.

"I'll have an easel and a stool for each of you. I'll send you a list of the paints and supplies you'll need. Each of you should have your own. You'll have to go to the art store in Tours. They're well stocked. But call ahead. They have weird hours. And you have to wait." He went back into the interior, and a few seconds later, returned with the painting of the French countryside over the mantle that Ingrid liked. He handed it to her. "For you," he said.

CHAPTER 10

Emergency House Call

1962
Miles

When Belinda Mae's staff-sergeant husband, Andrew, was assigned temporarily to Libya, her mother and sister returned to the States. Belinda Mae slid into lonely despair with only her two children for companions at their quarters in Châteauroux. For support and commiseration, Ingrid visited as often as she could.

One Saturday, late in the evening, Ingrid called Miles at home.

"Belinda Mae's thinking about suicide," she said.

"Belinda Mae?"

"That sweet, caring girl who was with us at Oradour-sur-Glane."

"What's wrong?"

"She needs help."

"She should go to the hospital, Ingrid."

"She won't go. She's got no one to stay with the children."

"Isn't there a neighbor who could watch them for a while?"

"I could go. But it's not that. She's afraid of someone at the hospital."

"Who?"

"I don't know. Would you go with me to help? She knows you. Ollie's at the Bumpy Landing. I'm worried."

Miles picked up Ingrid, and they drove to Belinda Mae's. When they arrived, the front door was open a crack. Belinda Mae lay on her side on an overstuffed sofa in the family room, a pillow over her head. She did not speak or respond when spoken to.

Supposedly, the children were in bed, but squeals with jabber and clatter with bangs came from the back rooms of the house. "Quiet the children," Miles whispered to Ingrid, who went to the back. He took an upholstered chair where he could watch Belinda Mae and sat looking at her. In thirty minutes or so, Ingrid returned. Belinda Mae had not moved. Miles put his index finger to his lips to signal Ingrid to be quiet. He pointed Ingrid to another chair close to him facing Belinda Mae.

After another fifteen minutes, Belinda Mae began to sob, her body trembling. Ingrid rose to go to her but Miles signaled her to sit down. With time, Belinda Mae calmed; she put the pillow to the side and turned, still full length on the sofa to look at Miles and Ingrid. It had been more than an hour and a half since they arrived. The children were finally asleep.

"How do you feel?" Miles asked Belinda Mae. She said nothing, and Miles held up his hand to stop Ingrid when she moved again to go to Belinda Mae.

They waited another ten minutes.

"I know it doesn't feel good," Miles said to Belinda. "But it doesn't last forever." He paused. "We're here to help until it gets better."

Belinda Mae sat up, holding her head with her hands, her elbows on her knees. She said nothing.

"This is a bad time. For your sake, let us take you to the hospital where there is always someone to help."

"The children," Belinda Mae said dismally.

"I'll find someone to care for the children," Ingrid said. "They'll be safe."

"I don't want to go."

"Why is that, Belinda Mae? Ingrid asked.

"You can tell us later," Miles said. "Just let me admit you until you feel better."

Belinda Mae withdrew into herself again, eyes closed, her breathing measured.

"What is it about the hospital?" Miles asked, not understanding why she would not go.

"Is there someone there you don't want to see?" Ingrid asked.

Belinda Mae retreated again, sobbing silently.

"Who is it?" Ingrid asked.

Belinda Mae leaned back on the sofa and closed her eyes again.

After another long pause, Ingrid said, "I'll stay with you in hospital so that whoever or whatever you're afraid of won't trouble you,"

Ingrid and Miles waited a few more minutes until Miles nodded at Ingrid and said to Belinda Mae gently, "Get your coat. Ingrid will stay here and find someone to care for your children. Give her your keys. I'll take you to the hospital."

"I'll come to stay with you as soon as the children are cared for," Ingrid said.

"And I'll be with you until Ingrid can come," Miles said. "Things will be better. We'll be sure of that."

Ingrid stayed with Belinda Mae in hospital for most of four days. On the fifth day, Belinda Mae had slowly responded to rest and medication, and she returned home.

That evening Miles had dinner at the Sterns.

Oliver spoke to Miles. "How did you learn to handle that crisis? Ingrid was impressed. Were you trained?"

"Nothing special."

"Well, pretty impressive, my man."

"I'm going to talk to Pamela, too," Miles said.

"Pamela?" Ingrid asked.

"Pamela Gardner. The chief of nursing service," Miles said. "She's great at what she does. And in a few days, I'll ask her to review the suicides we've had here. See if there are any patterns that might point to causes we might deal with."

Ingrid gave Miles a brief glance letting him know she appreciated what he was doing, that he was searching for the circumstances of Belinda Mae's agony.

"Have you had any suicidal patients, Oliver?" Miles asked.

"Like all of us, I probably see a new one every other week, and plenty that I'm following."

"Do you see trends?"

"They're all lonely. The longer we're here, segregated in this exhausted country, it will just get worse."

The next day Miles met with Pamela Gardner.

"We've had seven suicides in the last three months," Miles said after introductory pleasantries. "All dependents and all women. We need to find those in trouble before they act. Those with unwanted thoughts about killing themselves."

"It's hard to detect without knowing someone well enough to have their confidence," Pamela said.

"We should do surveys. I've outlined the questions. Search for signs of depression and despondency. Ask about melancholia, despair, sadness, discouragement. Do they have emotional swings? Have they lost the desire to do things? Do they have memory loss? Are they quick to anger? Is their marriage satisfactory? How do they feel about their children?"

"It's a good idea," Pamela said. "I can contact the director of nursing where I trained. She'd have valuable suggestions. How would we get the survey out?"

"We would give a survey to every woman who visits inpatient or outpatient clinics."

"Should it be wider than that? People who may never come to the hospital?"

"Maybe pass out surveys on the spot at women's meetings and functions at the commissary. Contact every dependent who arrives after, say two months, to see how they're doing."

"And how do we translate the results into prevention?"

"Education and providing services to those who need help. It will be mainly dependents. The military may not be enthusiastic, but I don't see how they can object. Everyone has been touched by the suicide of someone they know."

"And we need to have services to help the families who struggle with returning to some form of normalcy when they lose a loved one."

"I think we can make help available," Miles said. "I talked with the clinic and ward managers individually. They were enthusiastic. They deal with so many problems on a personal level and care about their patients, and they've felt the need for some action too."

"That's good," Pamela said. "I'll get the survey polished and to you for approval. I'll form a team to handle the distribution and collate the results. I'll keep you posted."

***

Miles called a meeting of GMOs. Specialists and flight-surgeons were invited, but only one responded. Springer was asked but did not attend.

"We need to address the suicides among the dependents," Miles began. "Seven in the last three months."

"That's not our job." Ravenel said. "We can't stop suicides."

"We have a responsibility, Jerry, for the well-being of our patients," Miles replied.

"Just words, man. It's crazy thinking. We focus on pain-free longevity. We're General practitioners, not shrinks."

Miles scanned the group. Pamela had warned him to prepare for resistance.

"We're a hospital without a psychiatrist or a clinical psychologist," he said. "And we need to identify those who have death thoughts, who worry about life's end."

"So how are we going to do that?" Captain Singh asked. "It would take hours grilling each patient for dangerous thoughts."

"And it would take hours to establish rapport to entice them to reveal inner thoughts they'd be ashamed of," Ravenel added. "None of us has the time."

"I agree about time," Miles said. "I propose that we survey dependents routinely with a questionnaire."

"So what? Who's going to follow up?" Aba Singh asked.

"Our nursing staff would be the first line. I've spoken to them, and they see it as a way to make a difference."

"Who would have the expertise? We need experts."

"I've asked the division commander if it's possible to have a psychiatrist or clinical psychologist assigned to Châteauroux."

"How did that go?"

"He said it's Springer's duty. And I've talked to Springer about bringing in experts from Orléans and Wiesbaden to train staff," Miles said.

"And?"

"Springer said we don't need experts and stop bothering him."

There was an I-told-you-so silence from half the doctors in the room.

"Look," Oliver said, "Miles is doing all the planning. You really won't have to do anything."

"I just need your support," Miles said.

Oliver looked around the room. "You have our support," Oliver said.

But Singh shook his head. "It's a waste of time, and the nursing staff will be swamped."

"Noted," Miles said. "I'll keep working to identify problems that arise. The survey should be functional next week."

"When you find someone suicidal, I still don't get who's going to intervene," Singh persisted.

"As I said, at first it will be nursing; later, maybe the patient's personal physician. Nursing personnel will establish contact and be a source of support by listening and sharing. And referring."

"A pipe dream," Singh said.

There was an extended pause filled with indifference from most.

"That's it," Miles said.

All stood and began to leave.

"Thanks," Miles whispered to Oliver.

"Handle Springer carefully." Oliver said to Miles. "He won't like an idea that's not his own."

Outside the room, George Pingree approached Miles. "It's a good idea," he said. "Springer will never accept it."

"Thanks, George. But I'm going to press on anyway," Miles said.

***

In the first two months of the survey project, there were no suicides among dependents. The success of the follow-up to the survey was evidenced by five admissions for observation in suicide-watch and twelve patients frequently visited at home by the nursing staff.

Springer, stating negative economic impact, refused to hire staff psychiatrist or psychologist, and he would not release funds to support visiting experts from other bases. He noted that claiming success of the project on surveys was not scientific and could, and probably was, due to chance. He ordered Miles to stop submitting requests for additional personnel that went above his head. He would make the decisions about staff on his own.

CHAPTER 11

Escape

1962
Miles

Three weeks later, Ingrid came to Miles's door before six in the morning.

"Belinda Mae killed herself."

"Oh, no."

"A neighbor found her. She'd sealed the doors and a window with masking tape and turned on the gas. A neighbor found her and called me. I saw Belinda Mae," Ingrid sobbed. "She was sitting in the kitchen chair slumped forward onto the table. The children collapsed in death, still clutched their toys at her feet. I feel terrible."

Miles could only imagine the depths of Ingrid's pain. Belinda Mae had been abused by life, and there was no rhyme or reason. "I wish we could have done more," he said, feeling inadequate. She cried, and he held her.

"It was worse than I knew. Her world had become complicated. She was pregnant."

"Andrew's been in Libya for months."

"She was forced."

"Raped? Who would do that?"

"She wouldn't tell me. She made me swear to never tell anyone that it happened, but now that she's dead . . . She feared retaliation as a liar. And she was convinced the military would do nothing to serve justice on one of their own. Regardless of guilt."

"She was probably right." Miles said.

"Is there anything we can do? She didn't want anyone to know. She was sure she would be the one to be blamed too, and nothing would ever be done."

"Let me make some inquiries."

"Don't reveal Belinda Mae's pregnancy."

"I understand. Of course not. "

"She never had a chance."

Miles looked into Ingrid's sorrowful, benevolent eyes damp with tears. "There was nothing more you could do," he said.

***

Miles met with Oliver in Oliver's exam room between patients.

"Belinda Mae killed herself. And her kids," Miles said.

"Yeah. Ingrid told me."

"Staff liked her."

"She'd always been a little jittery," Oliver said. "She told Ingrid she was raped."

"Do you think it was someone at the hospital?" Miles asked.

"I doubt that."

"Why would she lie to Ingrid? Belinda Mae hadn't told anyone else. And Andrew was in Libya. I'm sure she didn't tell him. He might always doubt the rape might have been consensual."

"Accusations of rape are tough to decipher," Oliver said.

Miles saw reluctance in Oliver's eyes just before Oliver quickly looked away.

"Someone in this hospital penetrated her against her will. And she became pregnant. She wouldn't lie. And it all adds up," Miles said.

"There's nothing in her chart about complaints or accusations."

"I looked too," Miles admitted. "But she was afraid to speak out. She knew nothing would be done if she accused someone specifically, and that she would be blamed for seduction. I hope it wasn't a doc."

"It's not a doc," Oliver said.

"How do you know? But no matter who, it's always he-said-she-said, and the male would always be believed blameless, and she'd be ruined," Miles said. "People are eager to think women are obsessed with seducing men."

"That's a little harsh, Miles. All of us are sensitive to possible accusations because of what we do. Examinations are intimate by the nature of the exam."

Miles shook his head. "Someone assaulted her," he said. "I'll ask around. See if anyone will know about rumors."

"Good luck, my man. But don't screw up your career for a bimbo."

"She wasn't a bimbo, Ollie. She doted on her family. She wasn't promiscuous. She was deeply religious."

"Andrew has been away for months without a break. She'd be wanting," Oliver said.

"I don't buy it, Ollie. I'm positive she was assaulted. She was not a seductress. Ingrid knows that too."

"Ingrid can be blind about people she likes. And she likes almost everyone."

"Belinda Mae was wronged."

"It's just hard to prove."

"Well, if we're right, it's happened to others, and it will happen again."

"You'll never find proof, Miles."

"If we know who's guilty, we can at least take some action."

"No military lawyer would touch such a case involving a dependent claiming rape."

"But there must be other ways than legal to prevent it."

The next day Miles met Pamela, the nursing supervisor. She was alone in her office. She asked Miles to sit.

"You knew Belinda Mae," Miles said, leaning forward with intensity.

"It's terrible."

"When I admitted her to the hospital, did you see her?"

"Every day on rounds. Twice I talked with her for a half-hour or more."

"Something happened that made her take her life. Do you agree?"

Pamela paused, obviously resistant to sharing her thoughts, her countenance grim. "Do you have any clues as to what happened?"

"I see presumed molestation of women often, to tell you the truth," Miles said.

"Sexual?"

"Always in some way flirting, touching, assaulting. And always with a cloud of innuendo."

"Do you know if it happened to Belinda Mae?"

"I never had that impression. And she always seemed so conscious of doing right that it would never occur to me."

"But you've heard about it?"

"Never Belinda Mae specifically. But she was an attractive young woman. It may have occurred. And certainly, she was assaulted. Why don't patients report it?"

"They do," Pamela admitted.

"To whom?"

"Me. Other nursing personnel."

"And what do you do?"

"I usually talk directly to the abuser. Military police aren't interested in dependents who get pregnant."

"Does that work?"

"I think so. Mostly, at least for a while."

"What if it continues to happen?"

"I report to administrative personnel. A few times I've gone to Springer when personnel advised it."

"What did he say?"

"He thanked me. Said he'd look into it."

"And nothing happened," Miles guessed.

"Nothing. I went back to him again with my concerns and he lectured me on the over sensitivities of women and their eagerness to accuse someone of rape for any reason. I told him that I wasn't talking about just rape. That sexual abuse is often subtle and not always assertive behavior. 'I can't act on a woman's hurt feelings,' Springer said. I was damned angry, and I said, 'It's more than hurt feelings, sir. It's degrading, demeaning, humiliating, and it affects a woman's quality of existence.' Without hesitation, he said to me, 'Dismissed, Lieutenant!' 'But, sir,' I countered. 'Dismissed,' he said again, almost yelling."

"I wish we had another commander," Miles said. "Is there someone else to go to?"

"I'm hesitant, sir. One of the accused was related to the commander. "His son," she said.

"Did you report it?"

"I can't chance a dismissal. And the commander would be vicious, especially with family involved. I'm career."

Miles thanked Pamela.

"Don't be too persistent, Captain," Pamela warned. "It could get vicious."

"I'm going to talk to the commander about Belinda's sexual assault. We all liked her. Would you go?"

"Yes. But just be careful."

Miles took Pamela to confront Springer with truth. He was sitting behind his desk in his office. He crushed a smoldering Lucky Strike butt into the aluminum-foil wrapper from a Hershey's chocolate bar.

"What you wanting?" Springer asked.

"It's not a want . . ."

"Sir, damn it. It's not a want, *sir*. Sit down."

"I'll stand—sir. Thank you."

"Out with it."

"A patient committed suicide. There's no doubt . . ."

"Belinda Mae Cerrone. I heard about it."

"There's no doubt it was despair over an unwanted pregnancy."

"My sympathies to her family. But women make mistakes sometimes."

"She was sexually assaulted, sir. The child was not her husband's."

"You can't know that."

"He's been on assignment in Libya. He hasn't been here."

Springer frowned, closing his eyes for a few seconds, and tilting his head. Then he looked at Miles. "Okay. So what?"

"It was someone in the hospital."

"Buckle up, Ballard. I don't want rumors circulating about my herd."

"Mrs. Cerrone was wronged. She deserves justice."

"It was her problem, Ballard. The woman was a slut."

"She was not a slut," Miles said. "Was she, Pamela?"

"No, sir. She wasn't."

"Bag that talk. She was my patient a couple times," Springer said. "I know."

You saw her with her children, Miles thought. *She was a terrific mother.* He looked directly at Springer, who did not raise his stare from the cigarette pack on his desk. Miles doubted Springer personally was a rapist, but he had a strong suspicion Springer knew the perpetrator. That made him an accomplice.

"There should be an investigation," Miles said.

Springer slammed his open hand on the desk; papers fluttered, and some fell to the floor. "Goddamn it. Stop stirring the pot."

"Whoever it is needs to be justly tried. Mrs. Cerrone deserves that."

"Look, Ballard. A woman gets pregnant. She claims assault. There is never any case to prosecute. And all women are flirts."

"That's not true."

"Sir!"

"Sir, she was a kind, moral, religious woman with a loving family. No way she enticed a man to rape her."

A prosecutor would make any accused airman a hero of the Cold War. He'd make the woman a prostitute. Find men who would testify against her. And the accused would go unprosecuted, Miles thought. *The world would believe the accused was enticed into consensual lovemaking by a wanting woman.*

"Cease and desist, Captain," Springer said. "I won't have scandal in my hospital."

"Something should be done," Miles persisted.

"Get out, both of you."

Miles and Pamela left to prevent another angry tirade from Springer.

Miles stopped by Ingrid and Oliver's place on the way home. Ingrid was alone; Oliver was still at the hospital.

"I asked Springer to call for an investigation," Miles said. "And he refused. Called Belinda Mae a whore-slut. Said no soldier should ever be prosecuted."

"Did he order you to not be involved?"

"In so many words."

"Did he know who the perpetrator was?"

"Ninety-nine percent sure. But he'd never say."

"Is there any justice in the military?"

"Not where Springer's concerned."

***

A week later, Miles saw Pamela at the commissary checkout. "Nothing has happened. Nothing will ever be done," Pamela whispered once they were outside. "She deserves justice."

"But she never reported anything. She was so afraid of what would happen to her."

"Would you testify to that?"

"I will. And more. I know who did it. She told me when I visited her. She was distraught. It was Springer's son Kramer, the one who fills the vending machines in the hospital."

"And you haven't said anything?" Miles asked.

"I promised her I wouldn't. She was adamant."

Even after death? I doubt she meant that.

"That boy should be punished."

Miles thanked her for her willingness to speak up.

Miles went immediately to Springer's office, but finally found him at the officer's club sitting at the bar. Miles approached. "We need to talk."

"Not here, Ballard. Come by the office tomorrow."

"At a table, then."

"Not in the mood, Captain."

"I know who raped Belinda Mae Cerrone, Colonel. And I'm going to report it."

"Tell the law. Leave me alone."

"It was your son."

"Christ, Ballard," Springer said with more irritation than anger. "What proof do you have?"

"I have a witness."

"Who watched a rape?"

"She knew Belinda Mae well. Belinda Mae told her."

"And that's it? Some broad says that a slut told she'd been raped by someone. My son, for god's sake? Come on, Ballard. Be real."

"It's not right. She was pregnant."

"And you can never prove the father. Even if it was a rape."

"I'm going to report it."

"You just do that, my friend. See how far you get with a dead victim who never reported or complained."

"She told a reliable source."

"That's not a victim's response."

"It should trigger an investigation."

"Wrong there. These accusations happen once a month. Few are investigated. And never by someone who heard from a friend that it was so-and-so. And if you want the investigation restricted, it will never get off the tarmac. Not with no evidence and a supposed-victim prostitute."

"That's not true. She told a reliable resource. I'm going to report it."

"I have to tell you, Ballard, you've got your head up your arse. You'll suffocate. And I'll be the last to grieve the loss of your miserable life."

Miles talked with Ingrid and Oliver the same evening.

"Springer's right, Miles. It'll never fly," Oliver said.

"Belinda Mae needs amends," Miles said. He resolutely believed it.

"Ollie's right," Ingrid said. "Belinda Mae never wanted her pregnancy known or her name to be associated with a pregnancy."

"It should be addressed," Miles insisted, "even just to try to prevent him from doing it again."

"Belinda Mae didn't want it. I think it's wrong to bring it out. It does more harm than good," Oliver said.

"Let's have a glass of wine and talk about the future and things we can do something about," Ingrid said. "And always keep Belinda Mae's injustice in mind. She deserves not to be forgotten."

And that's what they did, although Miles never accepted that Springer's son should go scot-free.

CHAPTER 12

The Medical Chart

1963
Miles

Although Major Schultz's first name was Cuthbert, since childhood he'd been called Reno—the Nevada city where he was born and raised. He was a C-54 pilot of long standing, a legend of sorts for his flights through the southern corridor during the eleven-month Berlin airlift of 1949.

On a Wednesday night after ten o'clock, he returned to Châteauroux from a six-day airlift of personnel to the Congo. He'd logged more than thirty-six hours of flying time and dreaded going home as tired as he was. He drove from the airport to Michelle's place near the Bumpy Landing to see Suzette, a woman who could comfort him. He woke her from a deep sleep, but she was glad to see him.

"A hard trip, eh?" she asked.

"Miserable. Glad to be back."

"Your wife, she is well, no?" Suzette asked.

"I haven't been home yet, Suzette. She's unhappy. She wants to return to the States."

"It is good for her to go, no? To be where she wants to be."

"I think I told you she's from Arkansas. The school here is much better. And because she married me, her family all but disowned her."

"I feel sad for her," Suzette said. Her compassion for Reno was weak. She knew she was rarely in his thoughts when he was away.

"And she hates being alone, even with the children."

As they shared a bottle of wine, Reno said, "She drinks, Suzette. I worry about her health."

He left Suzette's apartment near the Bumpy Landing for Brassioux after midnight. A light mist dimmed the yellow headlights required in France, and he could barely see details a few yards in front of him. The blurred image of a *deux chevaux* pulled onto the road from a side drive, he hit the front end from the side, spinning the car 180 degrees. His car careened across the road with minimally checked momentum. He tried to brake, but within seconds, hit a tree trunk head-on and was thrown out of the car into a mass of broken glass and mangled metal. He blacked out.

Gendarmes arrived. The French driver, seriously injured, was rushed to a local hospital. Because Reno, as an American was involved, military police were called, and a military ambulance transported Reno to Châteauroux air base hospital.

***

Miles was on in-house emergency call at the hospital when Reno arrived. As was protocol, initial assessment of injuries was completed by a trained airman, which took more than an hour. By the time Miles answered the phone, dressed, and walked to the ER from the on-call room, Schultz's wounds were sutured, X-rays taken, but medications withheld until Miles could complete a neurological evaluation. Reno sat on the exam table, his arms back for support, his legs dangling.

Miles introduced himself. Reno gave a slightly slurred greeting.

"I'd like to take a blood alcohol," Miles said.

"I don't want that," Reno said.

"That's your right. But it would help me establish a diagnosis and assist in providing the right medical assistance."

"Don't want it, Doc."

Miles recorded vital signs, listened to heart and lungs, tested reflexes with a rubber-ended hammer—ankle, knee, arms—and looked at X-rays of the two injured limbs and found no bone breaks.

Reno had difficulty remembering a few details, and his breath had a pungent whiff. When Miles asked again about possible alcohol ingestion, Reno said nothing, grinning as if he didn't understand. Miles tested the standard signs of driver impairment. He caught Reno when he fell sideways attempting to complete the heel-to-toe walk-and-turn test; Reno's horizontal gaze showed a slight nystagmus, and he could not perform the finger-to-nose test. Even two hours after the accident, he was unable to comply with the one-leg stand for more than a few seconds.

Miles admitted Reno to hospital for observation and completed entry of findings into Reno's chart.

The next day at ten o'clock he did a complete re-exam. Reno had no physical or mental impairment and was discharged.

Two days later, at fourteen hundred hours, an Air Force police officer knocked on Miles's closed exam-room door. Miles excused himself from his patient and opened the door.

"Captain Ballard?" the officer asked. Miles nodded.

"You're needed at the hospital."

"Now? I'm not on call," Miles said.

"Now."

"I have a patient."

The officer shrugged. "Commander Springer is out of sorts."

"And it's an emergency?"

The officer shrugged again and gripped Miles's left shoulder with enough authority to start him moving.

Springer sat behind his desk and told Miles to close the door.

"You treated Reno Schultz two nights ago. Was he drunk?"

"Can't say, sir. He was impaired after an automobile accident."

"You described detailed tests that showed impairment, and probable intoxication."

"They're in the chart."

"Look, Ballard. It's probable he was drunk when the accident went down and when you saw him. But you gotta change the chart."

"Why, sir?"

"I don't want anything about being drunk in there."

"There is nothing about being drunk. And I'm not comfortable with altering a medical record. It's a crime."

"Take out all that drink-test stuff."

"I can't do that. It's a required examination for the physician. Reno could have had brain damage, and it could be interpreted as malpractice if I didn't examine for it."

"But he didn't have no brain damage," Springer said. "I tell you, Ballard. The accident will be investigated; medical records will be reviewed. If it looks bad for Reno, even if there is only a *suggestion* he'd been drinking, it's over for him. What's in that chart will sink him. He could be discharged dishonorably, and he's damn close to retirement. It will end his career. He'll lose his benefits."

"I just recorded observations. No unfounded judgments."

"Investigators reading that chart will say alcohol intoxication. Pilots can't drink before a flight, drunk or not. And he was seen at the Bumpy Landing going to a call girl. Police know that. Men go to that place to drink. Change the note."

"It's a felony, commander. I could lose my license."

"I'm not asking; I'm telling you. It's an order."

"I can't."

"You can, and you will. I'll check that chart at five o'clock. Be sure it's done."

Angry about being intimidated by a superior he didn't respect, Miles went from the commander's office to Oliver's exam room door. When Oliver finished with the patient and was alone, Miles entered and closed the door.

Oliver looked up. "Hey, bro."

"You won't believe this," Miles said. "Springer just ordered me to alter a medical record."

"Really?"

Miles related the circumstances. "What would you do?"

"I'm not sure."

"It's illegal, Ollie."

"You can't be sure," Oliver said, "and I'd feel bad if Reno was sober and the accident was just an accident sans alcohol. That would be bad, man."

"We'll never know that truth. But he had symptoms of impairment."

"You did what's right. But the system makes judgments without considering facts or circumstances. It's an unspoken military rule. Never admit a mistake, and a comrade is always innocent."

"Still, I shouldn't have to lie for Springer. It goes against professional ethics."

"Springer's put you in a blind alley, man. He's the boss, even if he is a dung heap. Sad part, Reno's a regular guy."

"But I can't change a chart because my patient is a regular guy who made a mistake."

"Look. Worry about Springer's repercussions," Oliver said. "He's ruthless, and repercussions could be the pits for you. There's only the remotest chance that changing wording in a chart would come back to haunt you."

"It's not right," Miles maintained.

"Maybe you could get Springer to write his opinions. He could make an addition to the chart with his impressions from the evidence and commit his diagnosis, based on the chart, as his conclusion of no impairment. That's legal."

"He chuckled when I asked and told me to go to hell."

"Well, you're stuck. But you're right. Don't make any changes. Legal has ways to detect them."

"Thanks, Ollie."

"Sorry I can't do better," Oliver said.

Miles walked to the commissary and back, weighing what to do. Thirty minutes later, he was back in Springer's office.

"I can't do it, Commander," Miles said.

"Say 'sir,' Captain!"

"I can't do it, Commander, sir."

"It's your ass. You can do it, but you won't and that doesn't go down well with me. That's insubordination."

"I've done nothing wrong."

"You don't want to turn down a chance to help a buddy, Ballard. We're all in this together."

"I won't tamper with the law," Miles said.

"Watch your back, then, Ballard. Nothing good can come of this."

Miles left without comment. He took the bus back to Brassioux.

***

The next day, Reno's wife, Beatrice, in tears and trembling, her voice hoarse from shouting about Reno, was at Ingrid and Oliver's house. Ingrid sat reading in one of two aluminum lawn chairs in the yard. Beatrice collapsed in the empty chair before Ingrid could greet her.

"Reno will be punished for drunk driving, be dismissed, lose retirement, and refuse to support me and the children."

"What can I do to help?" Ingrid asked.

"I can't take it anymore." Beatrice broke into sobs. "Colonel Springer said Dr. Ballard could save Reno. Reno's been grounded until an investigation is complete. He'll lose incentive pay."

"I'm sorry," Ingrid said.

"You know Dr. Ballard."

"He's a friend," Ingrid admitted.

"It wasn't Reno's fault."

"Were there witnesses?"

"I don't think so."

"So what can Dr. Ballard do?"

"Say it was an accident. Reno wasn't drunk. That's all he has to do."

"Dr. Ballard didn't see the accident. And no one can know what definitely causes an accident, even if they witness it. Doctors treat patients. They're not lawyers. They don't make judgments on personal causes of happenings. I know Reno refused a blood test, but even if that had been positive, there is always the possibility this accident could have been caused by blurred vision from the fog, failed brakes, the Frenchman's not looking both ways."

"I just want to ask the doctor to do what's right."

"I'm sure he's done what's right—by the book. That's who he is. There he is now." Ingrid pointed to Miles's car preparing to pull into the drive. Beatrice ran to Miles as he got out of the car. "Dr. Ballard," she cried.

"Hello, Beatrice."

"Say he wasn't drunk," she blurted out.

Ingrid came up and said hello to Miles. "Would you like something?" she asked them.

"No! He's got to do what's right!" Beatrice screamed. "It was the frog's fault. Reno wasn't drunk!"

"Beatrice, I never said he was drunk."

"That's what Springer said."

"Come and sit down," Ingrid said to Beatrice.

"Bullshit," Beatrice screamed. She slapped Miles in the face, and his head thrust to the side. She slapped him again before he could recover.

Ingrid reached out to pull Beatrice from Miles, but Beatrice was taller by inches and fifty pounds heavier than Ingrid, and she broke away, backing toward the road.

"Please come in," Ingrid offered. "I'll make coffee."

Beatrice hissed, "I don't want your coffee," she said, and began running to her house.

After an awkward pause, Ingrid said to Miles, who was touching a red splotch on his cheek, "I'm sorry,"

"Apologies not needed—or warranted," Miles said. "She feels wronged."

"Come on in and relax," Ingrid said. "Ollie will be home in a few minutes."

Miles saw the Jaguar coming down the road and waited with Ingrid to greet Oliver.

Two days later, the airman from medical records called Miles.

"Sorry, sir, but do you have Major Reno Schultz's chart?"

Miles said he didn't.

"It's gone. Do you remember the last time you saw it?"

"I haven't seen the chart since the night I examined him. I left it in the exam room for a nurse when I'd finished making my entries. Ask her."

"I did. You remember that day, sir?"

Miles paused, "Last Tuesday night."

"Thank you, sir."

Miles saw Oliver in the cafeteria the next day. Oliver pulled him out of the dessert line.

"What happened?" Oliver asked.

"I refused to change the record. Springer cursed."

"Any assassination attempts?"

"A few threats. But the chart can't be found."

"My god. Where do they think it is?"

"If they had any idea, it wouldn't be lost," Miles grinned without humor.

"You think Springer, did it?"

"Don't you?"

"Given the timing of that chart missing, I think that chart will never be found. It's irrecoverable ashes scattered over the parking lot," Oliver said.

"I know you're right."

"I heard the driver of the *deux chevaux* died, but the French won't press charges. Apparently, it's tricky for them dealing with American military personnel."

"I'll probably be asked sometime to testify about the exam."

"It will all fade away, bro."

"The breathalyzer results are gone," Miles said.

"They're not valid evidence in court, anyway. Relax. Now you don't have to worry, my man. Reno will never be charged."

"I even had an anonymous death threat by phone last night. People do know," Miles said.

Oliver shook his head. "Let it pass."

"Not easy, my friend."

CHAPTER 13

Wayward Arrival

Fall 1963
Ingrid

Agnes Colletti arrived at Châteauroux in late 1963. She was the fifty-three-year-old unmarried sister of the light-colonel adjutant to General Read. Her mother had died, and she'd come to stay with her brother, her only living close-relative. Agnes was introduced to General Read, who insisted that Ingrid, as the best guide for newcomers, be assigned to her. Agnes requested a visit to Nohant, the home of the nineteenth-century radical feminist, George Sand.

Agnes, a Minnesota native, was overdressed for the season, wearing lace-up fur-lined hiking boots, cargo pants, and a down jacket. The clothes were loose on her slight five-foot, five-inch frame. She wore thick glasses that made her eyes look small, clip-on sunglasses, and a baseball cap that came down to her ears with "Phillies 1950" stitched in red thread on the front.

"You're a baseball fan?" Ingrid asked as they began the drive to Nohant in one of the three Packard sedans used by the military for tours.

"Since I was a little girl. It was time I spent alone with my father," Agnes said.

"What a special relationship," Ingrid said.

"Not really. He was a tyrant. A baseball game was the only time I ever saw him."

"Why 1950?"

"They won the pennant. But they lost the World Series in four games straight."

"Did you ever consider switching loyalty to a more successful team?"

"I should have, I guess. But I didn't go to games because I liked baseball. I liked that my father took me. He gave me some attention. After he died, I think the memories of going to a game with him gave me satisfaction that I couldn't find elsewhere. You a baseball fan?"

"Sorry to say, I've never been to a game."

"That's good. It's a slow, stupid game. I always took a book to read; I'd look up when my father said his favorite outfielder was at bat and with one swing could tie the game for extra innings."

"Did you request Nohant because you're a writer?" Ingrid asked. "Is George Sand a favorite?"

"I loved the translation of *The Master Mosaic Makers*. I studied French to read her original French version and bought a first edition when I was in Paris many years ago. Expensive but worth it. I'd like to discover her as a woman. She's made significant contributions to society as a feminist. And she struggled throughout her life with religion."

"Was she anti-Semitic? She lived for years with Chopin at Nohant, didn't she?"

"You're Jewish?"

"We are. And I know of Chopin's anti-Semitism. It must have been difficult for Sand."

"Chopin *was* anti-Semitic. But I've never known Sand's exact feelings. She seemed more focused on sexism."

"What do you write?" Ingrid asked.

"Oh, my. I'm not very focused. I would like to write fiction that reveals humanity in our age, creates meaning through story. And I've written nonfiction. All but two at an unpublishable level."

"Are you a teacher?"

"I've taught music and the history of music. Sixteen years."

"That sounds fascinating."

"It's what I love. As a vocation, not a business, to be sure."

Ingrid pointed out a farmhouse where same-day fresh eggs were always available. "Do you cook?" she asked.

"Minimally. My brother and I are hiring a chef for main meals, or else eating out."

"Well, even if only for breakfast and lunch, eggs from that farm are worth discovering. And I can recommend meat stores and bakeries. Being in farm country, produce is local and always fresh, depending on the season."

"You must cook," Agnes said.

"I do now," Ingrid replied. "I took courses in town. I never found pleasure in food preparation before. It was a burden to existence. But France made me curious as to how they've perfected food preparation as an art form."

They drove among vast fields of sunflowers, wheat, pastures for cows and goats, and fallow fields for horses to graze.

"Is there a Catholic church near the base?" Agnes asked.

"I've heard Saint-André in Châteauroux is popular with Americans. And there's a twelfth-century cathedral nearby in Bourges."

"Is that a long way? My brother is agnostic and doesn't go to church. I'd have to go alone."

"It's not a long drive. And the road is good too, the N151. We'll see it in Issoudun."

"And the French drivers. Are they dangerous?"

"A little wonky." Ingrid pointed to a vintage *deux chevaux*. "It's those little snail-paced two-seater tin cans that are annoying. And there are farmers' tractors on the road too. And oxcarts. They can be hairy."

"We've had our VW van shipped over," Agnes said.

"You'll be safe." Ingrid looked to Agnes. "We're going to visit the cathedral in Bourges on Friday. Roman Catholic. Would you like to go?"

"I think so," Agnes said. Then, said after an inexplicable pause, "Of course."

"Will your brother be available?"

"He doesn't have time since he arrived."

"I'll invite my husband's best friend, then. He likes to explore. So there'll be four of us. We'll have a tour and then dinner in the evening before coming back."

"That's good," Agnes said dismissively.

Ingrid was becoming more impressed with Agnes's eccentric but sharp intellect. But her ice-sculpture personality and sharp tongue, with often-failures to respond, brought on low expectations of enjoyment to Ingrid of the upcoming trip to Bourges.

***

A week later, on a Friday afternoon, Ingrid and Oliver introduced Miles to Agnes. The four of them started on an excursion to explore the Roman-Catholic cathedral of St. Etienne in Bourges. Miles and Agnes sat in the back seat.

"How was your flight in?" Miles asked Agnes.

"Tedious and terrifying. We refueled in Greenland and then again in Shannon. I'm not a strong advocate of flying. I spent hours in the toilet, the red 'X' light on the outside, mostly praying to survive."

"And your brother's a pilot?" Miles asked.

"Many years ago. He does mostly administration and consulting now for the General."

"But you still fly?"

"Of course. Flying means so much to him. He's very kind. He floods me with rational explanations on how safe it is."

They slumped into silence.

"This is our first time to Bourges for the cathedral," Ingrid finally said.

Agnes turned her head to Miles. "Do you enjoy cathedrals, son?"

Miles was surprised by the question. He hadn't thought about cathedrals, particularly. "I'm not very religious," he said.

"I hope it's all right," Agnes said to Ingrid, "that I called ahead. I have an appointment to talk with the senior organist at four o'clock."

"Do you know him?" Ingrid asked.

"Not personally. But he's famous."

"Was he surprised you called?"

"I'm Catholic. Good at the lingo. There's an international organist's group that meets annually . . . and keeps in touch."

"Hey!" Oliver said. "The men are here for the ride and a few beers in a café before dinner. "Right, Miles?"

"Sounds like a plan," Miles said, unenthusiastic about a few beers.

"And you play a pipe organ?" Ingrid asked.

"My mother thought music was my only talent. I know she was right. I studied with Arman Pedersen."

They arrived and parked. As they walked toward the entrance into the shadow of the cathedral's silhouette that immersed them.

It's an amazing structure, Ingrid thought. She gasped as they approached the entrance.

"You all right?" Miles asked.

Ingrid laughed. "Just astonished."

"It's a little overdone," Agnes said. "It doesn't look like a place where God might live. More like an emperor from a royal line of despots."

"On the weekends it's God's retreat," Oliver joked."

"This is so much more than I imagined," Ingrid said in reverence.

Miles gazed at the front of the structure—a Gothic cathedral with dual flying buttresses on a hill presiding over the city of Bourges. They approached the front five portals framed with large and small sculptures above the arched doors, illustrating the Day of Judgment, the punishment of the sinners, and the stoning of Saint Stephen. *They're so animated,* Ingrid thought. *And so many. So unique with life.*

"Ugly little creatures, aren't they?" Agnes said. No one agreed.

They entered the immense and unified interior space, a hundred yards long at least, Ingrid estimated, with soaring pillars in the vault.

"I think Notre Dame in Paris is better," Agnes said.

Ingrid felt the verticality of the interior to be transcendent, a unique sensation. "This is higher than Notre Dame," she said. "It's in the guidebook."

"But not as grand," Agnes admonished.

The preserved stained-glass windows filtered kaleidoscopic rays from the midafternoon sun and dispersed vibrant spectral colors around them. As a dutiful Catholic, Agnes knelt in prayer.

Oliver spoke to the group when Agnes stood. "Well worth the trip," he said, "but I'm up for a little refreshment while you go to your appointment, Agnes." He looked to Miles. "You be ready, my man?"

"Where are you going?" Ingrid asked.

"To a café for a beer. You women can join us."

Ingrid turned to Agnes. "May I join you on your appointment?"
Agnes nodded assent. "Of course."

Miles's growing fascination with the interior of the cathedral
made him want to stay. He hesitated, afraid to hurt Oliver's feelings,
but finally said, "I think I'll stay with the women, Ollie."

"What a bummer," Oliver said.

Inside, Ingrid, Agnes, and Miles studied the thirteenth-to-fifteenth
century windows that predominated the side walls of the cathedral.
After they explored the naves, they walked to a fifteenth-century astro-
nomical clock, the components larger than a small truck. A sign set on
a hand-carved music stand announced, "The clock was installed 1424
in a belfry-shaped painted case and bells chime on the quarter hour."
As if on demand, the clock chimed on the quarter hour and then again,
later, on the hour sounding the first four notes of the "Salve Regina."

It was time to keep Agnes's appointment with the organist—a
short, thin man, with disheveled white-hair and myopic, thick-lenses in
a silver wireframe. He spoke slowly and hesitantly with heavily accented
English.

"Two thousand five-hundred pipes were concealed in different
locations," he said, "the bellows that supplied airflow to the pipes, historically inflated manually, were now activated by a motorized blower
moving oscillated air to create sound. The organist demonstrated
fifty stops, four keyboards, and the set of pedals on the console that
immersed most listeners (and irritated others) in an ethereal, transcen-
dental embrace. The organist asked Agnes if she would like to play. She
was visibly eager but effused no appreciation. She had never expected
a Frenchman to be gracious. The organist retrieved slippers from a
cabinet for her to wear. Miles admired her confidence and total lack of
anxiety as she slid to the spot on the bench where she could reach the
most remote foot-pedals.

Her touch on the keyboards seemed magical as she played Bach's
Concerto in A minor. Tourists stopped to intently listen for a full twelve
minutes, the pedal swelling bass tones surging to the heights and nooks

of the cathedral's interior. Ingrid was moved to tears. Miles felt a unique awe for music he had never known before.

At the finish, Agnes entered a private discussion with the organist.

As they walked back to the Jaguar, Ingrid asked Agnes what the discussion was about.

"I asked him to tutor me on my improvement."

"And?"

"He said he'd ask the bishop," Agnes said.

Oliver waited at the car. Ingrid gave him a brief hug. "Agnes played the organ," she said to Oliver. "It was magical."

"I didn't know you were going to play," Oliver said to Agnes.

"It was highly improbable," Agnes responded.

Together, they walked to dinner.

The restaurant was quaint with a certain reserved elegance from another era. They sipped regional wine suggested by the sommelier. When Oliver asked, Ingrid gave him a brief description of the cathedral's crypt-interior.

"It's all overdone," Agnes said, "even for a Catholic."

It has a spiritual beauty, Ingrid thought. *Unique and inspirational.*

"Is the cathedral like being in a synagogue?" Miles asked Ingrid.

"It's different," she said. "The cathedral gave me a unique feeling of limitless extraterrestrial space."

"But how does it compare to a synagogue?" Miles added.

"I find the cathedral less reverent in some ways. Growing up with the Jewish faith is a cultural, humanizing experience. It was different in the cathedral. The cathedral lacked the feel of humanity that I feel in synagogue most of the time, even if there are only a few worshipers there. But each area of worship has its own effect on me. The cathedral tends to be reverent by an expansive display of space and artistic achievement. I felt awed at the grandiosity to which I had never been exposed."

"I felt it too," Miles said.

Ingrid continued, "Catholicism is probably an individual experience of connecting with God in a distinctive, personalized way. I'm not sure I can explain."

"Is Judaism a more communal interaction with God? Is that what you mean?" Miles asked.

"I think that's . . ." Ingrid began.

The clamor of two US military police entering the restaurant caused a sudden silence among the patrons. Heads turned. The police surveyed the diners, then walked directly to Oliver and Miles, their boots pounding the wooden floor, breaking the persistent apprehensive-quiet of the intrusion.

"Ballard? Stern?" the older policeman asked.

Miles and Oliver raised their hands.

"Return to base."

"Why now? What's up?" Miles asked.

"The president's been shot."

"The president?"

"President Kennedy," the police sergeant was near to shouting, exasperated and impatient. Nearby customers gasped. Ingrid's eyes dampened with tears. "Communists," Agnes accused without knowing.

"Is he all right?" Ingrid asked.

"We don't know."

"Where?" Miles asked.

"In Dallas. All medical personnel have been ordered to the base hospital. We've got others to track down."

As the police thudded to the door, the Americans were silent with concern. Finally, straining for relevance, Miles said to Oliver, "We'd better be moving."

The women stood and prepared to leave. Miles took bills from his wallet to leave on the table.

"No, *monsieur*," the owner said, "You do not pay. We grieve deeply for your president."

"Thank you," Miles said.

The women were ready. As they walked toward the door, the owner pressed a bottle of red wine into Ingrid's hands. "With our condolences, *Madame*," he said and backed away as a chef in a toque opened the door for their exit.

More than one third of the diners stood in respect for the Americans.

***

At the hospital, staff and personnel prepared for an onslaught of injured from a possible Soviet nuclear attack. Commander Springer told Miles to go to command headquarters and be prepared to treat the General for any medical emergency.

When Miles arrived in the command room at headquarters, the General merely waved acknowledgment of his presence and returned his gaze to a blackboard where a lieutenant was recording times that officers from a contingency-response wing would report to fly a requisitioned military C-135, a plane that would be in the air twenty-four hours a day. In the event of attacks on military installations, assigned specially trained personnel would restore the Châteauroux air station to a fully functional facility. Operation Mohawk. Miles was included as essential personnel and would be, when required, on flights with the General.

Jack Ruby shot Lee Harvey Oswald dead, and American intelligence investigated possible Soviet involvement in the assassination plot; Oswald's involvement with Russia as a CIA agent was suspected. The base remained on full alert for more than three months.

PART THREE
1964

CHAPTER 14
The Scheme

1964
Emily

In Boston for more than two years, Emily Lodge's life with husband Parker became a vacuum of caring and, in quiet moments, she felt trapped in a lonely, depressive existence. Parker's privileged existence left him with no need to be liked among the elite who had accepted him from birth, and he socialized with a few old cronies without her. He rarely talked to her or even looked at her. She felt transparent in his presence.

One day in May, Parker carelessly left an itinerary for Paris on a table in the foyer in Boston; Emily found it by chance and the next day asked if she could go with him.

"No!" he replied. "Don't bring it up again."

In her bedroom, she stripped to bra and panties and slumped into bed. She sulked for hours with a blanket covering her head, her mind stagnant with wounded dignity. As night approached, Parker entered the house and her determination to go to Paris drove her to action.

She opened the door to Parker's private study. "I want to go," she said. "I deserve to go."

He looked bemused. "Not possible," he said, chuckling straight-faced. He found her boldness absurd.

She cursed him, called him a son of a bitch. He rose from his chair, and before he was at full stance, she slammed her fist on his desk, intentionally knocking over fresh flowers in a crystal vase that fell splintering and scattering over the hardwood flooring near his feet.

He said nothing, his face devoid of emotion. She stopped to regain control of her thoughts, gasping with short, quick breaths. He sighed. "You're pitiful."

"I'm your wife. Treat me with the respect I deserve."

"You're not who you think you are, my dear."

"I'm more than you think I am."

"It's business. I will be totally occupied."

"I want to get out of this shithole. Pretend for a few days that I exist!"

His face was impassive. "I would not have time for you."

"You've never had time for me, for Chrissake. What's the harm in taking your invisible wife on a trip?"

"Get out," he said.

She stood her ground.

He walked to her, grabbed her arm, and forced her out the office door.

She went to the foyer. His flight itinerary was still there. On the kitchen phone she booked the same flight on the same day. She wrote down the details.

She went to his office and threw her itinerary on his desk. "I'm going," she said.

He gave a short laugh.

"It's not funny."

"You're out of line, woman."

"I'm at the head of the line. Don't you ever forget it."

He uttered a cruel, deriding laugh.

She flashed him a stiff middle finger.

***

Emily could not suppress a sliver of optimism for an enjoyable transatlantic trip with Parker. But she was denied a requested upgrade and Parker lounged in first class. She was in tourist. When they arrived in Paris, Parker was indifferent to her, and she trailed behind him to his hired private car. At arrival at the Hôtel de Crillon in their two-bedroom suite, ever hopeful, Emily asked if they could tour France together.

"No!" he snapped.

"I'll go by myself."

"I don't care what you do."

"I can't drive around France by myself."

"Jesus Christ," Parker said, exasperated. With only partially concealed anger, he arranged by phone for a car and driver for Emily for a month.

"Please come with me," Emily asked quietly.

"I've seen enough of France for a lifetime," he said.

She felt diminished again.

Unable to shed the ignominy of traveling alone, for two days she stayed in the suite and came close to panic from claustrophobia that she'd never experienced before.

On the third day, she booked a bus tour in Paris through the hotel's travel desk. But in the early afternoon, bored and uninterested, she left the tour and took a taxi back to the hotel.

On the fourth day, she sought out her driver and demanded that he map out routes to castles. He suggested the Indre department. That afternoon, she visited Château de Valençay before arriving in Orléans and listened to the history of Joan of Arc. She was not impressed. That night, at dinner alone in her hotel, she looked at maps in her *Michelin* guide for Châteauroux, where she knew Miles was stationed. By early afternoon, she'd registered at a hotel in Châteauroux and went to the base hospital before 1600 hours. She pushed her way to the receptionist's window, squeezing in front of a young woman and her aged parent at the head of a line and asked for Doctor Miles Ballard.

"Are you a patient?" the receptionist asked.

"Oh, no. I knew him in Boston."

"Your name, please."

"Emily Lodge," she said.

"I'll tell him you're here," the receptionist said without smiling. She wrote Emily's name on a notepad and tore off the top sheet to take to Dr. Ballard. "Have a seat."

Emily took a seat. A woman with two small children entered the waiting room and a uniformed officer stood to meet them. He seemed pleased to see them.

Miles entered the waiting room five-minutes later, his face impassive until he smiled hesitantly with recognition. "Em!" he said, "what's brought you to Châteauroux?"

Emily gripped his extended hand with determination. "Parker has business in Paris. I came to explore France." She couldn't decipher his emotions. At least he didn't seem displeased.

"I'm between patients."

"Do you have time for a quick coffee?"

He nodded.

In the hospital cafeteria, Miles ordered coffees and croissants and they took seats at a small round table for two.

"Where have you been so far?" Miles asked.

"Paris," she finally said, unable to remember the names of castles she'd been to that day.

"A good start. There's so much to see. Where are you going next?"

"Nothing planned. I decide day by day."

"And how's the family?" Miles asked.

"Unchanged," she said.

"Do you get to see them often?"

"I do visit Maine when the weather's good. Do you remember Mother?"

"Not often," Miles said with a weak smile that he regretted when she frowned. "Why do you ask?"

"It's okay. I wish she'd never said those things about you when you were in the attic."

"It's water under the bridge, Em. She wanted what's best for you."

But it wasn't the best for me, she thought. "I'm glad to see you," she said.

Miles asked about her work.

"I quit my job at Smith last year," she said.

It was beneath my deserved status as old Boston elite.

"Don't you miss it?" he asked.

She hesitated. "I never liked recruiting students for a mediocre college," she said.

"What are you doing now?"

"I keep busy. I'm assistant to the secretary of the Junior League now."

A nurse in uniform came to the cafeteria door and waved for Miles to follow.

"Look, I'd love to hear more, but I've got to get back to patients," Miles said. "Why not join me for dinner? I'd like you to meet two friends. We're going to try a restaurant near Issoudun."

The invitation surprised her and her spirit soared; she was sure she'd captured his interest again. "What's the address?" she said. "I have a car and driver."

"We'll pick you up at your hotel."

"Oh, good," she said. But she really would rather have been with him alone.

Oliver drove the Jaguar sedan. Miles introduced Oliver and Ingrid as he assisted Emily into the back seat and joined her.

She talked of her life in the States. "Oh, there are lots of benefits," she said. "Parker belongs to the Knickerbocker Club for exclusivity, but he spends most of his time at the New York Yacht Club. Thirty-years ago he raced in the America's Cup. But he's too old now. Five of his six aging crew buddies are still alive and stay at the yacht club."

"Do you go with him to New York?" Oliver asked.

"I'm way too busy. Parker donated another hundred-thousand dollars for me to serve on the board of the Boston Museum of Fine Arts. It's a prominent position. Having Parker Batten's wife as a member gives them the prestige they all crave. And it boosts fundraising."

They arrived at Des Petits Pois in less than an hour.

Throughout the meal, Emily told of her family's house on Beacon Hill that had been in the family for four generations, or maybe five, she couldn't remember. And how her father, when he semi-retired, had leased the house to the lieutenant governor and now they stayed at their

Maine house year-round. Yes, her father had been a college professor, she answered when asked.

As they finished dessert, Ingrid asked, "Do you like France?"

"It's quaint," Emily said.

"Are you here tomorrow?"

"I can be. Yes."

"If you like, we could visit Château de Montsoreau."

"Is it a long trip?" Emily asked confidently, now that she had her say and they seemed impressed.

"A few hours," Ingrid said.

"We'll take my private car."

After dinner on their way home, Oliver and Ingrid dropped Emily off at her hotel and Miles at his Brassioux duplex.

Alone again, Oliver asked Ingrid, "What possessed you to invite her to go with you tomorrow? She's impossible."

"I think she's trouble for Miles, Ollie. I want to know why she's here."

"There's nothing you can do."

"I'm not sure. But still, we should try."

"What if Miles is still in love with her?"

"That would be terrible. I hope he's not."

"Don't mess with squirrelly love, Ingrid. You're not a *shadchan*. Keep out of it. Let them work it out."

"Miles is still vulnerable, Ollie. His story of her turning him down moved me."

"Don't get into it."

"If she entices him in any way and things go wrong, Miles will suffer. And if we do nothing, we'll be partially to blame."

"Not at all!"

"Emily Lodge can hurt him again. He doesn't deserve to relive pain by her."

"What if we misjudged her?" Oliver said. "What if she might be a shriveled lonely soul beneath all the meisms, fake kindness and caring without an ounce of remorse for what she did."

"She's got an agenda, Ollie. I don't think it's love. I think she's trying to erase her loneliness by snagging Miles again."

"It doesn't sound like she planned to come to Châteauroux," Oliver said.

"At best, it was unconscious at first. But I really think she's here to see Miles, not the local châteaux or cathedrals."

Oliver nodded in agreement. "Okay. Just don't deny him a true chance at happiness, Ingrid."

"He'll never find happiness with her. I'll find out what she's about tomorrow to be sure of her motivations. I won't let our friend be hurt." *I think of Miles daily,* she thought *and miss him when he's not nearby.* But she could never speak her mind, knowing Oliver could never accept the truth. She no longer loved Oliver as she once did, but it would be impossible for her to separate herself from him. She had committed, and with marriage, she owed him loyalty and companionship.

***

The next day, the sky was clear with a slight chill in the air. Ingrid thought Emily's hired Bentley sedan ostentatious as she rode with Emily in the back seat imitating English royalty. The driver kept the windows up continuously adjusting the heating system to comfortable temperatures. Ingrid missed the leisure of fresh country air.

"Do you really like being in France?" Emily asked.

"I do," Ingrid said. "I think you'll like it. Do you enjoy traveling alone?"

"Oh, no. I would never travel alone on purpose," Emily said with a rare divulgence of the truth. "Parker doesn't travel for leisure, and he won't take me on business trips. This is an exception. I insisted."

They remained silent as the driver passed a truck on the narrow, unmarked country road.

"The drivers are horrid here," Emily said when they were safely past the truck.

The sliding glass panel between the driver and the back seat was open, and Ingrid knew he could hear everything they said. Had he taken offense?

"Does your husband like France?" Ingrid asked.

"There's little Parker likes," Emily admitted. "To be frank, he comes to shoot birds and wild boar with friends, although I don't think he's ever bagged a boar. He's a shitty husband. He doesn't care for me. He married me because he—wrongly—thought my father still had his inherited fortune, and he needed a young wife for social events and political advantage."

"I'm so sorry," Ingrid said sincerely.

"I've no need for sympathy," Emily snapped.

"It doesn't sound like a rewarding life," Ingrid said, annoyed by Emily's sharp reply.

"Being on the board of the museum is my duty to Parker, but it uses up my time. I know nothing about art. But Parker is determined his wife will be regarded as the best fundraiser on the board, so we make a substantial contribution every year in my name."

"I've enjoyed the museum," Ingrid said. "I've been there twice."

"It's famous. But drab, outmoded art, don't you think? Do you *really* like it?"

"I do."

"Do you paint?"

"Yes. Whenever possible."

"I admire your industry. I think being an artist is menial work with essentially no reward," Emily said.

"I don't agree," Ingrid said. "Great art has its rewards to the artist and the beholder. I admire how the French treasure art and beauty in their culture. It's not just the visual arts, either. It's music, dance, cuisine, architecture, language. The value of art is instinctive for them."

"I can't remember most works of art. They all just blur together," Emily said.

They entered a town. From the front seat, the driver pointed out a small twelfth-century cathedral where the priest was a distant cousin on his mother's side.

They rode in silence for a few more minutes.

"Does Miles have friends?" Emily asked.

"It's one of the advantages of being a doctor in the military, Emily. Almost everyone is healthy, and doctors have time that they never would have in practice in the States. So they do make friends."

"But is he in a relationship?" Emily asked.

Ingrid remained silent.

"Well? Is he?" Emily persisted.

"I'm not sure." Ingrid avoided that Miles rarely dated. "Something happened in the past," she said. "I think he's afraid it could happen again."

Emily hesitated, her jaw clenched, her face hardened. "You know, don't you?"

Ingrid deliberately looked out a window.

"He told you, didn't he? That nerd."

"It's not important," Ingrid said.

"He told you about our engagement!"

Ingrid remained silent.

"What did he say?"

"He mentioned it, Emily, that's all."

"And you think I was unjust, don't you? You think I was wrong. I didn't have choices, you know. My parents. His past. Did he tell you about that?"

"I don't make judgments."

"He comes from no-status parents."

Ingrid didn't respond.

Emily took time to control her thoughts. Finally, she said, "Would Miles be open to a relationship?"

Ingrid delayed her answer. "I think he's satisfied with life as it is now," she said.

"But is he happy with someone?"

"He seems happy with almost everyone he knows."

"Damn it, Ingrid. He must be lonely?"

"He works hard. He's a dedicated physician. He doesn't have time to be lonely."

"Working to excess. That's exactly what I would expect. It's what my mother told me about him. He's a victim of his profession."

"That's not Miles. He's not a victim. He looks to the future. He's content, and I think he covets discovery."

"I made him content once," Emily said. "I could do it again."

"You're married now."

"To the wrong man, goddamnit."

Ingrid mentally shrugged and stayed quiet.

"I need to talk to him again!" Emily said. "Just find a way to get us together again. That's all I ask."

"I'm sorry. I can't do that."

"You won't do that, and you tell me you're his friend. Why not?"

"It's not my place."

"Damn it. There's nothing wrong. I just want to talk to him."

Ingrid did not respond.

"Look. If it's money you want, I'll pay you. Anything you ask," Emily said.

Ingrid exhaled. She waited. "That's insulting," she finally said.

"What's insulting?"

"Offering money," Ingrid said.

"Don't be so condescending."

"I'm offended."

"Money's what you people want." Emily reached into her purse and took out a small stack of bills. "Take this. I'll give you much more later if you do it."

Ingrid shook her head. "You're impossible."

"You'll regret it," Emily said.

"I don't think so."

"It's so little to ask."

"It's more than I will do."

Emily's breathing increased. "Jew slut," she said.

Ingrid couldn't look at Emily. She needed to be far away. She leaned forward to the driver. "Turn around," she said.

"That's not for you to tell him," Emily said. "He's *my* driver."

But the driver had already turned into a side road to make a three-point turn.

"Damn it. Go on!" Emily shouted at the driver. "Go to the Château whatever-it-is."

"Yes, madame." In seconds, he'd completed his turn and was headed back on the route to Châteauroux instead of Château de Montsoreau. "*After* we take the lady back."

Silence pervaded on the return to Châteauroux. Ingrid left the car without a farewell.

Emily went to the hospital, but Miles had left. The receptionist didn't know where he was. *She knows, but she won't tell me,* she thought angrily. "He's a doctor. How in the hell do you find him when you need him?" she asked sharply.

"He's not on call," the receptionist replied.

"I'm a friend from the States, not a patient. Where is he?"

The receptionist was silent for a moment. "Probably at the officer's club."

"What's the number?"

"I'll try to reach him for you."

She was back in thirty seconds. "He's not there."

"Will he be in the hospital tomorrow?"

"Yes, ma'am."

Emily left without a thank you. The military frustrated her.

***

That evening, Oliver returned home from the hospital to Brassioux at half-past eight. Ingrid was in the spare room on a high stool at a slanted drawing board, drawing caricatures of friends from photos, celebrities from magazines, and famous historical figures from statues.

"Good day?" she asked as Oliver entered and gave her a kiss on the cheek.

"Hideous. One of Springer's patients committed suicide."

"Where?"

"In her hospital room."

"That's unbelievable. No precautions?"

"There is a suicide protocol. But typical of the military, it was in place but not used. And Springer never spends enough time with patients to know what they're feeling. She stockpiled drugs she stole from the nurses until she had enough to kill herself."

"I hope it never happens to one of your patients."

"Always the chance. How was the trip with that fiend of a woman?"

"For a while she acted casually coincidental, but she's here to snare Miles."

"Did you find a single shard of virtue?"

"None, really. She called me a 'Jew slut' when I wouldn't take money to arrange a contact with Miles."

"What a bitch. Has she left?"

"She's determined. She'll hound Miles. He needs to tell her to go away. He's too nice. She'll destroy his capacity to love," Ingrid said.

"No, Ingrid!" Oliver said, irritated. "Stay out of it. No matter what you do, good or bad, Miles would never feel the same about you or me if you meddle. And he's a good friend."

Oliver's tone of voice disturbed her, but now was not the time to object. She'd do what needed to be done on her own.

***

The next day, Emily woke before six, bathed, dressed, and ate the complimentary hotel breakfast—coffee and a croissant with quince jam. She was determined to go to the base to find Ingrid Stern. She'd slept poorly believing by offending Ingrid she had squandered an opportunity to achieve reconciliation with Miles. Now she was determined to succeed.

At the base hospital, the receptionist gave her the Stern's address in Brassioux.

There was no answer at the door. As she walked back to her hired car, a woman stepped out of a neighboring house and waved. "Can I help you?" she called out.

"I'm looking for Ingrid Stern."

"She won't be home for a while. She teaches a yoga class for wives at the gym on Mondays."

The driver found the gymnasium easily, and Emily walked in through the door to the basketball court. Twenty-one women on individual mats were spaced out on the floor in three rows. Ingrid led the instruction from a mat in front of the students. Emily sat on the first tier of wooden bleachers to wait for the session to end.

When the women dispersed, Emily walked quickly and directly to Ingrid, who was rolling up her mat.

"I don't want to see you," Ingrid said.

"Please . . ."

"I'm serious, Emily."

"I'm so sorry, Ingrid. I wish I'd never said those things. That wasn't who I am."

Having listened to Emily's relentlessly acrimonious tone of voice now for two days, Ingrid ignored her false contrition.

Emily's woeful faux gaze looked down and away. "I just want to talk to him for a few minutes."

Ingrid hesitated. She wasn't rude by nature, and she waited for Emily to finish.

"I want advice," Emily said, "and you're the only person I know in France for more than just a greeting. Just a few minutes. Could we sit on the bleachers?"

Ingrid shrugged, eager to be rid of her.

They sat, separated by two feet, looking straight ahead as if neither at the moment, wanted to discover the other's thoughts. Finally, Emily turned her head to look at Ingrid.

"Last night I was alone in the hotel and I hated myself. I'm not a shrew, Ingrid. Maybe I've become one. But that's not the real me."

"Why do you need me?" Ingrid asked.

"I'd like to spend time in France . . ."

I knew it, Ingrid thought.

"I would like to talk to Miles again. Let him know how I feel. Ask him to forgive the past."

"Why did you turn him down, Emily? He thinks he wasn't up to your family's standards. Your social standards."

"That was mostly my mother. I wasn't mature enough to know how vicious she can be. And she denied me to love him. She thought he'd never satisfy me, thought life required me to find a companion with the wherewithal to marry, survive, and procreate in Boston. And that was stupid, of course. I had no thoughts about what marriage would be like, or what I wanted a husband to be. And I was impatient."

"Afraid?" Ingrid asked.

Emily hesitated. "That was part of it."

"Of what? Commitment?"

Emily paused. "I don't know."

Maybe you don't know how to love. "And you want him now?" Ingrid said.

"I think he really loved me, Ingrid. Probably because he didn't know who I was at that time. I've changed. I didn't know it then, but living with a husband like Parker has made me understand how precious Miles's feelings were."

Emily was a liar, and Ingrid didn't want to hear about her feelings. Emily could never love Miles with the devotion he deserved. Any possible feelings for others were directed inwardly to herself.

"I want to spend a while here in France, knowing who Miles has become."

"He doesn't want to see you."

"You can't know that. And I can make him content again."

"Do you love him, Emily?"

"I do."

"Even though you haven't seen him since you've been married?"

"I've been alone at times, sustained by what Miles was to me and I didn't recognize."

"Well, underneath his back-to-business exterior, he's a kind person," Ingrid said. "He's sensitive and cares for others. And I don't think he'll allow himself to be hurt again."

Emily teared.

That isn't real, Ingrid thought. She said, "You're married."

Emily cried for a few seconds and wiped tears from her face with her coat sleeve. "It's not a marriage, Ingrid. It's never been consummated, and Parker spends his time with his men friends."

He's gay, Ingrid realized. *And she's unwillingly chaste.*

"Would you help me get close to Miles?" Emily continued. "I can learn about France. He might spend time with me."

Ingrid sighed. "I've no desire to be involved."

***

The next morning, Ingrid walked to Miles's Brassioux duplex at half-past seven. Miles was in his pajamas.

"Relax," she said, knowing his propriety.

He invited her to step inside, out of the cool morning air.

"I think you should talk to Emily," she said as they stood facing each other in the hall.

"Why?"

"Do you still care for her?"

"Never."

"Can you tell me honestly that you felt nothing when you saw her at the hospital for the first time in more than two years?"

Miles frowned. "For a few seconds, maybe. I was surprised to see her. And, yes, there was a moment of pleasure from memories of our times together before."

"But after that, nothing?"

"Nothing."

"Be honest. If you have the faintest love for her still," Ingrid said, "admit it and tell her. It's important. She wants to stay here to recapture the old times." *It would be a disaster for you*, Ingrid thought. *I hope you see that.*

"I don't want that. It's past. She can never be in the future."

"Well, then, you must tell her. I don't like her. But she's so desperately lonely. She's searching for someone who cares. And to continue to believe she can regain it with you could ruin her. She has to let go of the dream—face the nightmare disaster of her marriage and go on with life. She's going to find you very soon. Be ready to treat her with sympathy and caring but free her to get her life on track for a realistic future. Be firm and convincing. Tell her your feelings one way or the other."

"I don't owe her anything." Miles said, frowning.

"Just tell her. It's a critical gesture to help another human being."

The next day, before dawn, Emily demanded her driver park in front of Miles's duplex. After a few minutes, when a light went on in the house, she sprinted up and rapped relentlessly with the brass knocker.

Miles opened the door, tying the sash of his wool robe around his waist. He'd had a sleepless night; Ingrid's words had made him anxious.

He looks exhausted, Emily thought. "Hear me out," she said.

"I don't have time, Emily."

"Let me in!" She entered before he could speak. She positioned herself a few feet away from him. She felt the need to embrace him, to establish intimacy through contact, but she hesitated, afraid of what he might do or say.

"I'm sorry for the past, Miles. I wish we could start new again."

All night he'd struggled with this confrontation. He did miss the times when he adored this woman, dreamed of spending his life with her—and he hadn't been entirely truthful with Ingrid. But now, looking at Emily, he felt nothing for her. And he could never forgive her. She had to move on in life without him.

"Don't say anything more, Emily."

"Don't say that!"

"We will never have a life together."

"How can you be so cruel!" she cried. "Damn it. You still care for me."

"I don't, Emily. And I never will." He was firm. He rejected every inclination that he might ever want to be with her again.

"I love you," she said, "You can't ignore that. You're all about yourself now. You'll never find anyone like me. Never. You don't deserve me. You're blind to what I could do for you." She flushed, breathing deeply, and close to shouting, her voice harsh and ratty.

Miles held the urge to respond. To defend himself. He was not at fault. She was inadequate in so many ways.

He opened the door. "Leave, Emily."

"Don't you dare throw me out," she yelled.

"Just leave. You're not welcome."

"I hate you! You arrogant, selfish, son of a bitch."

He reached for her elbow to usher her out the door.

"Don't you dare touch me." She started moving out onto the path. She hesitated and turned slightly to look back, but Miles was closing the door.

Indignant and angry, she walked to the car. "Paris," she said to the driver.

She went straight to her hotel. Parker was not there. She made arrangements for a flight, packed, placed a note on the hotel bed, and left early the next morning for home—angry, sad, lonely, and shaken at the prospect of her uncertain future.

CHAPTER 15
D-Day

June 1964
Alyce

Even after more than two years in France, Alyce avoided dinners at the General's and his wife's whenever possible, she still didn't like her mother's company or her cooking. But this was a Sunday evening, and her mother seemed desperate to have a family gathering with two guests—a base chaplain and his wife.

Even with three family and two guests around a rectangular dining table headed by the General, the conversation was plagued with long pauses as each of them stared intermittently at their plates and arranged their ground beef, mashed potatoes, and peas into individually unique piles as justification for not looking up at others.

"Are you going to the D-Day commemorative on June sixth?" Alyce asked the General.

"We're going," the chaplain offered when the General paused in a response a few seconds too long.

"Of course, I'm going, Alyce," the General said, incensed at her slight of his importance at the affair. "It's the twentieth."

"I was on the first wave," the chaplain offered.

"Pointe du Hoc for you?" the General asked the chaplain.

"Thank god, no. Near the Brits on Gold."

"What was a chaplain doing in the first wave?"

"I was a corporal, sir. Before seminary."

"I was in the 82nd airborne," the General said, with conceit. "C47 Dakota. Second 'Boston' wave."

"You piloted soldiers?" Alyce asked.

"Twenty-eight paratroopers, four crew."

"Were you hit?"

"Rudder damage and lost a starboard engine. We were at a thousand feet and took a lot of flak until we were past the beach, and we dropped to seven hundred feet for the jump."

"I wanted to be a paratrooper," the chaplain said. "But I'm near-sighted. They turned me down."

Alyce raised her hand for the General's attention. "I want to go to the ceremony next month."

"The General has his own plane," her mother said.

Alyce glared at her for repeating with pride something that everyone knew, and many didn't approve of. "Can I go with you?" Alyce asked again. "I'd like to do an article for the paper. Eisenhower's going to be there."

"I'm one of the hosts." The General scoffed at Alyce's failure to again sound the respect he thought he deserved.

"Did you know Eisenhower?"

"Met him twice after the war."

"Could you help me get an interview with Eisenhower?"

"Absolutely not."

"Because I'm a woman?"

"Because you're a journalist."

"He's going to be interviewed by CBS's Walter Cronkite. Could I at least watch that?"

"That will be private."

"Don't bother your father," her mother said. "Have your editor ask the president's staff," she added. "The General's not going to be involved in giving you permission for interviews."

"How would I make contact?" Alyce asked. "It's impossible without help."

"Don't try," the General broke in, "it will never be possible."

"I'm a journalist on the staff of the *International Herald Tribune*. That should mean something."

"The General worries that journalists misrepresent the truth," Mother said. "He doesn't want to annoy people."

Alyce tensed, her body rigid, and glared at her mother. "Journalists are accurate with facts, Mother. It's how we're trained and it's what Generals and politicians fear! Facts!"

The General frowned, his gaze distant to the ceiling somewhere above the chaplain's wife.

"Tommy doesn't want to be judged unfairly," Mother said. "It's easy for you journalists to take down successful people in high places."

"Only the high and mighty," Alyce said. "Those with false pride and conceit."

"Tommy's not like that," Mother said vehemently.

"I'm speaking overall," Alyce said.

"I don't want you to use my status to get your way," the General finally said. "Not now or ever."

"Could I just fly with you up and back? That wouldn't be wrong."

A silence ensued as everyone at the table stared at the General, trying to anticipate his answer.

"Let her go, Tommy," Mother said.

After a pause, the General shrugged, which everyone took as agreement. The chaplain's wife excused herself to go to the "ladies," unsettled by the tension that had saturated the air.

Alyce could not suppress a sardonic smile at her mother. At least she had a spot on the General's plane.

The General's DC-3 was perfect for flights in the European theater; it landed on short runways. The General had fitted it with a galley for food and drinks, and plush seats that reclined halfway to horizontal.

Alyce mounted the moveable steps to enter the door behind the wing and made her way down the aisle. The General sat alone at the bulkhead in the first row of single seats. She saw an empty aisle seat in the row of double seats over the wing. She stored her handbag in the overhead compartment and sat next to Miles in the window seat without asking if the adjacent one was occupied. She buckled her seat belt and turned to Miles. "My doctor!"

"You must be in the peak of health," Miles replied. "You've never been in for a checkup."

"Too busy," she said.

He nodded and reached for the newspaper in the seat pocket in front of him.

"That's my paper," Alyce said.

"Sorry," Miles said, handing the paper to her, even though he'd brought it on board.

She laughed and pushed the paper back toward Miles "No, no. I mean that's the paper I work for, the *International Herald Tribune*. That paper belongs to you."

Miles laughed. "I forgot you worked for the *Tribune*," he said.

"Freelance," she admitted.

"Are you going to see the president?" she asked.

"I go where the General goes, like a seeing-eye dog."

Miles looked out the window as the right engine cranked up. The noise increased. Then the left engine. Miles watched the ground crew directing the pilots to the taxiway. He was thankful when the whining roar of the engines stifled conversation. He wasn't in the mood for conversation with Alyce; he didn't feel good with the after-effects of a lingering cold.

They reached cruising altitude.

Alyce reached under the seat in front of her to retrieve a book she'd brought, *The Autobiography of Alice B. Toklas*. "Have you read this?" she asked, showing him the cover.

Miles shook his head.

"Alice B. Toklas was the lifelong partner of Gertrude Stein. They lived in Europe and during the war were Nazi sympathizers of the Vichy Regime. Both were friends of the French General Pétain, who was sentenced to death for treason by French courts after the war. Stein thought Hitler merited the Nobel Peace Prize for Mein Kampf. Both Stein and Toklas were Jews and lesbians, and it's thought that their pro-Nazi defense was probably what protected them from death in an era when Jews and homosexuals were slaughtered by the Nazis as undesirables. You should read it."

"I'd like to," Miles said.

"And pass it on to Ingrid. It would expand her knowledge of the Holocaust."

Alyce leaned toward the window, half over Miles's lap. The wing blocked most of her view. "Where are we now?"

"We've got about an hour and half left." Miles closed his eyes and put his head back against the headrest.

When they landed in Évreux, the passengers gathered inside the waiting area for transportation from the Air Force base to the coast. Alyce walked up to Miles in the crowd.

"Look," she began, lowering her voice in the crowded room. "You're my doc, and I need a favor."

"I'm not sure . . ."

"Just listen. It's not much. My father wouldn't help me get an interview with the president. He wouldn't even help me get in to see the interview with CBS and Walter Cronkite."

"I don't think he has . . ."

"You're with him the whole day. I've got this handheld tape recorder. It'll fit in your medical bag." She pointed to the black leather bag in Miles's left hand. "Could you keep it? If you get into the president's interview with Walter Cronkite with my father, could you just switch it on?"

Miles was silent, stunned at her audacity.

"It's no skin off your nose."

"Go ask your father. If he says yes—if it's allowed and he tells me it's okay—I'll think about it."

"You know he won't approve."

"You're right."

"It's not illegal."

"It's not right. And it may be illegal."

"All I want is a little help."

Miles shook his head. "Don't ask again."

The General walked up to Miles an hour later when the dignitary's transport arrived to take them to quarters. "I say, boy, you don't have any tape recorder with you, do you?" the General asked.

"No, sir!"

"Don't lie to me. I'll put you in lockup."

"I won't lie."

"And don't listen to that daughter of mine. Major Tsitsipas overheard her."

Alyce spent the morning interviewing veterans. She talked to a German vet who had been in the bunker at Pointe du Hoc on D-Day. She asked him how many had been killed that day. "Not enough," he said and turned and spat on the ground as he walked away.

In the afternoon, at the Pointe du Hoc, as a member of the General's family, Alyce had negotiated to sit in the second row of dignitaries. Her father was one of the Generals who gave a brief presentation about his experiences. He praised the bravery of the more than four hundred and thirty pilots, copilots, navigators, and radio operators who flew C-47s in from the west to drop paratroopers behind the beach frontal attack. He spoke of his ditch in the sea and who had died on that dreadful day.

"And the living heroes of my crew," the General continued, "are here today: copilot Jake Palmer and navigator, Harold Sessions. Stand up, guys," as he led more applause.

The fool. He totally ignored the solemnity of the occasion, Alyce thought, embarrassed that he was her father, and not her real father at that, and would dwell on his contributions, ignoring the immense worldwide impact of hundreds of thousands of soldiers. She was surprised when copilot Jake Palmer, who was sitting next to her in the dignitaries' section, stood. She'd never seen him before. She leaned toward him as he sat down. "I'm from the *International Herald Tribune.* May I interview you when the session is over?"

Jake smiled, "Off the record?"

"Not exactly what I wanted, but yeah, okay."

More speeches about bravery, sacrifice, heroics, and injustice continued. Then President Eisenhower stepped up to the podium. He delivered a heartfelt talk about the horrors of the day in his strong mid-American accent. His words mesmerized Alyce, and toward the end of the speech, he gave a memorable thought, a thought she would never forget:

> Dwight D. Eisenhower.

> ". . . This D-Day has a very special meaning for me. And I'm not referring merely to the anxieties of the day, anxieties that were a natural part of sending an invasion where you knew many hundreds of boys were going to give their lives or be maimed forever. But my mind goes back so often to this fact.
> "My own son graduated on D-Day from West Point. After his training, on the very day he graduated, these men came here, when the British and our other allies stormed these beaches . . . for one purpose only . . . not to gain anything for ourselves, not to fulfill any ambitions Americans had for conquest . . . but just to preserve freedom, systems of self-government in the world. Many thousands of men have died for ideals such as these, these young boys over whose graves we have been treading, looking and wondering about their sacrifices, they were cut off in their prime; they have families that grieve for them that they never knew the grave [significant] experiences to go through of life, like my son [has known]. I devoutly hope that we will never again see such things as these [again].
> "I think, hope, and pray that humanity has learned more than we had learned up to that time . . . . Every time I come back to these beaches, or any time I think about that day twenty years ago, I say once more: we must find some way to work for peace and to really gain an eternal peace for this world."

An interesting man, Alyce thought, feeling even worse about her father's dwelling on his own experience and ignoring the liberation that took hundreds of thousands of lives.

The seats cleared, and Alyce stayed with Jake Palmer in a now empty row of chairs.

"Eisenhower's speech moved me," she said.

"It was a terrible time," Jake said.

"What was it like for you? You were in the first wave. Was it frightening?"

"It was the second 'Boston' wave. More than four hundred C-47s wingtip to wingtip approached from the west at about one or two thousand feet because of the dense cloud cover. We took a lot of flak at that level. We carried twenty-eight paratroopers for a drop at six hundred feet behind the front lines. We lost a wingman minutes before we were to drop. There were a lot of heroes that day."

"The General once said you lost a starboard engine and rudder control."

"That isn't exactly true, ma'am. We wouldn't have survived that day with an engine lost. One out of three planes from our squadron was shot down. But we made the drop without major damage. In the confusion of poor visibility, radio silence, and obscured landmarks, we dropped the paratroopers two miles from the DZ."

"The drop zone?"

"Yes."

"What did you feel during those moments?"

"We were all afraid of death. But I really had no time to think about the act of dying."

"You weren't shot down over France as the General said?"

"No, ma'am. The General was a captain then. He doesn't remember what happened. We ditched in the channel, out of fuel from a leak in a fuel tank. Teddy, our radio operator, was last out of the plane and was dog paddling toward us when the General went berserk as Harry Sessions, the navigator, and I were trying to keep his head above water. When the General saw Teddy, he thought he was the enemy and he grabbed a piece of floating debris and hit him in the head, knocking him unconscious. By the time we got the General quiet enough that one of us could take care of him, I swam to Teddy, who was half submerged, face down. When I turned him over, he was dead. He'd drowned before I could get through the rough waters to revive him."

"And the General doesn't remember?"

"No, ma'am. He'd been psychotic from the time when the wing man was hit and went down in flames—the General was moaning and cursing and babbling. Harry pulled him out of the left seat so he wouldn't bang the controls."

"And you flew the plane?"

"Yes, ma'am, until we had to ditch."

"The General received the Medal of Honor for that mission," Alyce said.

"For the traumatic effects of battle, I guess. And that's justified. He was hospitalized for a couple months and then sent to the States for electric-shock treatments. At least I was told that a couple years later by Harry the navigator. He's here today."

"Yes, isn't that him?" she pointed to a man a few seats down the next row. "I saw him stand when the General called on him."

"You can ask him, but I've never heard him speak about that day. It's sad; Teddy and Harry were the heroes that day, but Harry doesn't believe the General deserved a medal . . . but he never speaks about it."

My father is a sham, she thought.

She continued the interview until Miles approached to escort her—at her father's request—to the airport for the return trip in the General's plane.

Alyce wrestled with what she should do about the truth about her father. It was difficult being around her mother now. Did her mother know? Alyce wasn't sure. And it would never be wise to confront her father. He would not remember the day, and if slivers of remembrance of the day did come to him, he would suppress them never to be considered again.

She decided to never publish the truth. It would serve no purpose after almost twenty years.

***

When Alyce returned home from Normandy, Margaret, her sister, had arrived from the States, fatigued, and bordering on non-communicative from the trip and months of wrangling over a still-unresolved divorce settlement. Her children were in her husband's custody, and she no longer cared. She was ready for a new life.

Margaret and all her belongings were in the second bedroom that Alyce had been using. Alyce's belongings had been relegated to a corner of the dining room, and she was to sleep in the living room now on the pullout sofa bed.

Alyce, Margaret, and their mother sat at the small metal-top kitchen table bearing a coffee pot and three mugs. An awkward silence prevailed for many seconds.

"Alyce went to the D-day commemoration in Normandy to hear father speak," her mother finally said. Margaret remained silent, doing her nails.

"Did you have a good trip?" Alyce asked Margaret.

Margaret shrugged.

"Please try to be civil, Margaret," Alyce said. "Make a little conversation."

"Don't trouble Margaret, dear," Mother said, looking down at her coffee cup, annoyed at Alyce's remark.

"We're living together. Is it trouble to speak when spoken to?" Alyce questioned Margaret.

"Don't be unreasonable. Margaret will talk when she is ready," Mother replied.

"Will the two of you shut up," Margaret said. "I have a splitting headache."

I can't take this, Alyce thought. She left the table, grabbed her coat from a peg near the front door, and went for a walk.

CHAPTER 16
Pamplona

1964

One evening, at Ingrid and Miles's weekly painting session with Bruce McKenzie, the subject focused on still-life renderings of a decorative pottery-bowl filled with oranges, avocados, figs, apples, and in the foreground, along with four brown eggs, asparagus, and a sunflower all set on a polished walnut tabletop. Ingrid said to Miles, "Ollie wants you and me to go to the San Fermin fiesta in Pamplona. The running of the bulls. Like in The Sun Also Rises."

"It's dangerous," Bruce said sternly.

Ingrid smiled. "I won't be in the running. But I can enjoy the festival with thousands of others."

"Just be careful around bulls," Bruce said. "Each day the run lasts about two minutes, so there's lots of time to enjoy the festival without running with the bulls."

"Can you go, Miles?" Ingrid asked. "I'm going to ask Alyce Read, too."

"Sure. Tell me the dates."

"I'll send you a note. Ollie can order your costumes."

"How are we supposed to dress up?" Miles asked.

"I'm not sure yet. The traditional costumes are the same for everyone. White shirts and pants and red waistbands and kerchiefs. Not mandatory, but natives and most visitors wear them," Ingrid said. "Alyce and I will decide when we get there."

"Is running with bulls for you, Miles?" Bruce asked.

"I'm not sure about running with bulls."

"And Oliver?" Bruce asked Ingrid.

"He's intent on doing at least one or two during the week."

"Not good for amateurs," Bruce said. "The village men practice for years to stay in shape. They study the bulls to scout out peculiarities in their movements."

"I know," Ingrid said. "And Oliver isn't in great shape. Or even athletic. But there will be no stopping him."

"It's not an easy trip," Bruce said, concerned about the risks to his friends.

"How long?" Miles asked.

"To drive? Five hundred miles. Eight to nine hours."

"We could go by train, couldn't we?" Ingrid asked.

"That's a disaster. Fifteen hours, two changeovers en route. Expensive. You'd do better to drive."

"We'll drive," Ingrid said. "It will be a great trip."

"Perfect," Miles said.

Bruce frowned.

The next morning, Bruce mentioned it to Ina over breakfast. "Ingrid and Miles are going to the running of the bulls."

"Camargue?" Ina asked.

"No.

"Arles?"

"Pamplona."

"Well, that will be the most exciting. Is Oliver going?"

"It was his idea. And they're asking Alyce Read."

"Don't worry. They'll be all right."

"I'm not so sure," Bruce said. "Oliver seems intent on running with the animals and I worry about him. I don't know about Miles, but I think he's got too much good sense to run. Pamplona has the best-bred bulls raised for exciting kills. Amateurs are really the only ones at serious risk."

"Are Oliver and Ingrid getting along well?"

"It's hard to know."

"She spends a lot of time with Miles."

"They care for each other, Ina. I don't think either of them knows the strength of the other's feelings."

"Is it love?"

"I think intensely platonic now. But I think each has a passionate caring for the other."

"And Ingrid's unhappy in her marriage?" Ina asked.

"She'd never admit it. She's extremely loyal to Oliver as a husband and the institution of marriage. I'm pretty sure she is faithful to Jewish laws and traditions of marriage. But Oliver doesn't seem to respect her."

"She's such a kind person," Ina said.

"I feel terrible for both of them," Bruce said.

***

Three weeks later, Ingrid and Oliver, and Miles with Alyce, left before dawn for the drive to the Pamplona festival. They stopped at a small restaurant north of Bordeaux for lunch, and an hour and a half later, they crossed the Spanish border. A beezeless, gentle, misty rain obscured the rolling hills and the architectural features of the stone buildings in the farms and towns. The windshield wipers slapped back and forth rhythmically.

"I'm not really comfortable with this bull thing," Ingrid admitted.

"What's wrong now?" Oliver said.

"I asked a travel agent in town. He thinks it is unnecessarily cruel. They breed bulls for the ring, torture them, and usually murder them if they don't do a superior job at the climax of the performance. It's bizarre."

"There's plenty to do at the festival," Oliver said, "You'll be on balconies to watch the run and you don't have to go to the bullring at the end of the run.

"You thinking about running?" Oliver asked Miles.

"I wouldn't enjoy it," Miles said.

"It's the challenge. You don't have to *enjoy* it."

"Not for me, Ollie."

"But you're going to watch, right? I got us coveted balcony views on the route."

"Of course," Miles said.

Ingrid asked Alyce her thoughts on bullfighting.

"I don't understand it. But I'd like to learn. I'll take photos and do interviews. The *Tribune* is interested in an article with personal standpoints of participants and observers."

"It dates back to the fourteenth century," Oliver said.

"How has it lasted this long?" Ingrid asked. "There must have been objectors."

"It is strange," Alyce joined in. "It's tied to a religious holiday in some historical way that I've yet to understand. It honors a saint who was the first Bishop of Pamplona. The red kerchief at the neck is to remember the saint's beheading."

"There are always animal rights objectors," Oliver said. "But they just demonstrate. There's no danger."

Miles, knowing Ingrid's feelings against hurting animals, gave her a sympathetic glance.

They rode in silence for a while.

By midafternoon, as they were approaching an intersection, Oliver asked Ingrid to check the map. "I think we turn soon. Did you see a route marker? We're on the A63."

"Have you seen a sign?" she asked.

"Not yet."

"Ah, I found it," Ingrid said, her finger on the map. "Look for the 121-A."

When they arrived in Pamplona, the sun was halfway to the horizon, dimmed by occasional sinuous clouds. Tourists crowded the streets. They found the Hotel La Perla.

"What were you thinking, Ollie?" Ingrid asked in amazement. "We can't afford a five-star hotel."

"It's close to the action."

"I'm paying for the hotel rooms," Miles announced, anxious about the antagonism building between Ingrid and Oliver.

"And we'll cover other expenses, then," Ingrid said.

Ingrid and Alyce went shopping in town intent on matching the traditional white and red costumes Oliver had bought for himself and Miles. At one point, through a store window, Ingrid saw a dark-haired woman who looked familiar, seemingly waiting for someone. She gestured for Alyce to follow, and they approached the woman.

"Hello," Ingrid ventured. "You look familiar. I'm Ingrid Stern. Are you from Châteauroux? My husband is stationed at Châteauroux air base."

"*Excusez, mesdames.* I speak English not well."

"You're not from Châteauroux?" *I know I've seen her before,* Ingrid thought.

The woman shrugged her shoulders and shook her head.

"I'm sorry to have bothered you," Ingrid said, turning with Alyce to walk away.

"I think she probably speaks English with perfection, don't you?" Alyce said.

"I heard no trace of an accent in those few words."

"Why would she lie?"

"I think it was in the commissary," Ingrid said.

"Would she be allowed in the commissary?"

"A guest can sometimes get a one-time pass."

"The French can be so rude. I thought you were more than gracious."

"Let's get dressed for the festival," Ingrid said. "I think we were wise to buy pants."

"Even if they were made for a Buddha," Alyce smiled.

Later in the day, as Ingrid gazed from the hotel window at the crowd, she thought she saw the woman again. She seemed alone, strolling hesitantly, as if without purpose.

When Ingrid and Oliver had a few seconds alone, Oliver was immediately grumpy. "Why are we paying everyone's expenses?"

"This was your invitation."

"Not for Alyce."

"I invited her, which effectively means *we* invited her," Ingrid argued. "And Miles is very generous to pay for the rooms."

"Don't ever say we'll pay again; ask me first. Always!"

Ingrid looked away, her eyes simmering with irritation.

Oliver had reserved two adjoining rooms with attached balconies to view the spectacle of the bulls and the steers and people careening through narrow cobblestone streets. He'd join Ingrid, Alyce, and Miles when he was not running. On the third day, he left early for the run and to be in the best position in front of the bulls. The others couldn't see the start or the first part of the run, but they heard the rocket launch and the roar of bulls and humans thundering down the course.

Forty-five seconds after the start, the runners came into view, cramped into a spaceless mass in front of the bulls. Oliver lagged from the leaders and had become enveloped by the pack, trapped behind a bull he could barely keep up with and nudged by the head-down horns of the bull behind him.

"Shouldn't he be outside the pack?" Ingrid asked anxiously.

"He's down!" Alyce shouted.

Oliver was on all fours and instantly turned on his right side. He tightened his body, chin down with arms over his head, knees drawn up to his chest—what he remembered from his brief instructions. *I'm going to die*, he thought. The front right hoof of a mid-pack bull trampled his thigh; he screamed. The next bull straddled him. A distance between the six fighting-bulls and the second pack of six steers, left a few precious seconds free of clamoring hooves, and Oliver crawled on hands and knees, dragging his injured leg, to the side of the course where two uniformed emergency workers lifted him to safety, below and out of the sight of Ingrid, Miles, and Alyce.

"We've got to go find him!" Miles said.

Within two minutes they were on the street headed for the flags above an emergency station where attendants and an ambulance were waiting. They approached.

"Oliver Stern?" Miles asked an attendant.

Two attendants were working on Oliver. He breathed oxygen through a mask attached to a tank. A woman stood by him, holding a blanket. *That's the woman from the store*, Ingrid thought. Alyce glanced at Ingrid, having noticed her too. The woman handed the blanket to the nurse and held Oliver's hand in both of hers. When she saw Ingrid and

Alyce she turned away, covering her face with her kerchief, and running into the crowd who had gathered in a half circle a few feet away.

Ingrid approached and leaned over to speak to Oliver. His eyes were half closed. "Ollie," she said with unrestrained panic.

But Oliver was flaccid and barely responsive.

"He is unconscious almost with pain medicine," an attendant said with a heavy accent.

"Do you know that woman?" Ingrid asked.

The attendant shrugged his shoulders.

"What sedation has he had?" Miles asked.

The attendant shook his head and said nothing.

The stretcher with Oliver was lifted and pushed into the ambulance.

"Where are the car keys?" Miles asked Ingrid. "Does Ollie have them?"

"In our room. On my bedside table. Here is the room key," Ingrid said.

Miles took the key. "Go with him to the hospital," he said to Ingrid. "Alyce, come with me."

"I'll go with Ingrid," Alyce said.

"You can't; they'll allow only one family member."

The woman, who had been at Oliver's side, stood at the edge of the crowd, her eyes wet with concern, and trying to hide her face. Neither Miles, Ingrid, nor Alyce saw her again. But Ingrid was suspicious of the intimate gestures she had witnessed. She knew Oliver had had affairs during their marriage. But she had not recognized, or maybe suppressed signs, since they had arrived in France.

The ambulance pulled away, lights flashing, siren and horns blaring.

"Will he be all right?" Alyce asked as they rushed back to the hotel.

"I'll get the keys and check out," Miles said. "Grab what you need and I'll meet you at the car." *I'll need directions to the hospital,* he worried.

***

At the hospital, X-rays showed a fracture in the femur and hairline cracks were visible in two lower-left ribs but no sign of lung collapse. Oliver's gaping thigh wound had been closed and dressed. Ingrid stayed with him at the hospital for two nights for blood transfusions. Alyce and Miles returned each night to the hotel. On the third day after the injury, with one day still left in the festival, Miles drove the Jaguar on their return to Châteauroux. Alyce sat in front, and Oliver lay on his back on the back seat. Miles had purchased three pillows from the hotel checkout and Ingrid positioned herself in the narrow space available in the back footwell.

Alyce and Miles could hear Ingrid and Oliver's argument. It started as soon as she asked if he were comfortable.

"Don't start," Oliver said.

"Do you need me to adjust a pillow?" Ingrid asked.

"Stop it."

Ingrid remained silent.

"I know you think I deserved this," Oliver said. "I shouldn't take risks."

"What are you talking about? I feel terrible it happened, Ollie."

"And you think I should have listened to you—you and your superior intelligence always knowing about everything. I'm not mentally retarded, you know. You're not always right."

"I've never thought . . . "

"Don't blame me for the inconvenience. I didn't try to get hurt."

In the front seat, Alyce glanced at Miles, who shook his head slightly in disbelief.

"It's not an inconvenience," Ingrid sighed. "It's a terrible accident of unpredictable fate."

"I don't like condescension."

"Rest for a while."

"Don't bully me! I'll rest when I want to."

Oliver's labored breathing calmed after a few minutes and a silence descended in the back that lasted more than a hundred miles.

CHAPTER 17

Insubordination

1964

In April of '64, Colonel Springer court-martialed Miles for insubordination and failure to abide by Uniform Code of Military Justice. Miles tracked down the lawyer Bob Goggin. "Did you hear what happened?"

Goggin stood and leaned against the rake he was using to aerate the soil in the garden behind his house in Brassioux. "Of course. It's all over the base."

"What should I do?"

"You'll be allowed to plead guilty or not guilty. If you plead guilty, the commander can dismiss or impose a punishment. But you should plead not guilty. A panel will review the evidence before a jury is convened, and I think you'd be vindicated in a trial."

"Can I have counsel?"

"Yeah. A defense attorney. Military or private."

"Would you do that?"

"I'll have to look, but I don't remember a medical doctor being court-martialed for insubordination. As military, I probably have as much background as any counsel; I'd have to be appointed."

"I wouldn't trust anyone else," Miles said.

"I'll see if I can get it worked out. If I can, I'll do the best job possible."

"Thanks."

"On one condition," Goggin said.

"Name it."

"I win the next two out of three squash games. I want to make my wife proud."

"Agreed."

"And don't go around saying how difficult it's going to be to lose to me."

"My voice is silenced."

***

Miles submitted a plea of not guilty. When the trial ensued, the prosecuting attorney brought up Miles's continuous refusal to call Commander Springer "sir." Goggin pointed out how trivial that was and that Miles had learned and now routinely called Springer "sir."

The prosecutor felt that among the worst occurrences for insubordinate disobedience was Miles taking a proposal for training of triage, which had been ignored by Colonel Springer, to his commander for implementation and funding. "Humiliating," Commander Springer had testified.

Then, after a break, Oliver Stern was sworn in and brought to the prosecutor's table.

"I would never have thought this would happen," Miles said to Goggin.

"He was subpoenaed," Goggin responded.

The prosecutor approached Oliver in the witness chair. After routine questions, he asked, "Did you accompany Captain Ballard to Commander Dillinger's office?"

Oliver nodded.

"Speak up," the prosecutor admonished.

"Yes, sir," Oliver said.

The prosecutor established the purpose of the visit was to seek support and money for training doctors and personnel in case of nuclear attack. "Did you support that request?"

"I'm always in favor of more current training. But I was not in favor of going to Commander Dillinger."

"Why was that?"

"Captain Ballard is my friend. I admired the work he'd done on creating the proposal. I wasn't sure it was financially wise, but I thought the results would benefit doctors. I did not support going to Commander Dillinger."

"But you were there in Commander Dillinger's office?"

"I thought there was value to the proposal and hoped Commander Dillinger might support it. But I was apprehensive about bypassing Colonel Springer."

"That's a bummer," Goggin whispered to Miles.

"Because of Ballard's disobedience of Colonel Springer's reputation and standing?" the prosecutor asked.

Goggin objected.

"No matter," the prosecutor said, as his statement was removed from the record. He continued: "Do you wish now that you hadn't gone?"

"Yes sir. I wish I hadn't gone."

"Was Captain Ballard aware of your feelings?"

"Yes, sir, I expressed my concern more than once."

"He's your *friend?*" Goggin whispered to Miles.

"I thought so," Miles replied.

The prosecuting attorney continued. Miles was accused of continuing the suicide questionnaires after Springer had ordered him to stop because of costs and waste of staff time that diminished their performance. Goggin pointed out that the suicide rates among dependents had been among the highest in any branch of the military, and after the implementation of the techniques there had been a dramatic decrease, from two or three a month to zero for six months. The prosecutor asserted a measurable decrease in productivity among staff as a result of the questionnaires. Goggin insisted it was impossible to attribute decreased productivity to the effort to eliminate suicides.

The adjutant General called the lawyers to the bench. He looked mostly at Goggin. "Insubordination does not relate to suicides," he said. "The question at hand is directly related to disobedience of a superior's orders. That is unrelated to the success or failure of the suicide initiative. Understood?" Reluctantly, Goggin had to agree.

After a delay, the prosecutor presented an airman witness who said he heard the colonel's orders to Ballard. In cross-examination, Goggin asked the airman exactly what the colonel had said, "Did he say, 'I order you never to do another survey on suicide symptoms'?"

"Uh, not exactly like that."

"What exactly did he say, then?"

The airman seemed not to be able to look at the court; his gaze fixed on a crack in the wooden flooring.

"You're testifying under oath about something you can't quite remember?"

"No, sir. It was different. Like, it didn't make sense to do surveys on dependents about suicides. That it wasn't cost efficient."

"Did Colonel Springer say to Captain Ballard, 'I order you to stop'? Did he use that word, 'order'?"

"I don't remember that . . ."

"You just heard the colonel speak about the negatives of the action?"

"Well, it's hard to remember . . ."

"Did you hear the word 'order'? Yes or no?"

"I can't say."

"You do know you're here to testify about insubordination. How did you know Captain Ballard was out of line? What did he do that made you believe he was insubordinate?"

"He continued to do the surveys."

"And although you didn't hear an order given, you believe what you heard about the Captain, and you then saw over many weeks, if not months, what you thought was inappropriate action on Captain Ballard's part."

"Uh . . . I thought . . ."

"You assumed."

The airman descended into silence.

Back at the defense table, Miles leaned over to Goggin. "How did that go?"

"Not sure. He'd been coached for hours."

"I don't ever remember an order being given."

"Forget it. We've got a lot more to bring out."

The next day the prosecutor bought more instances of insubordination. Failure to "correct the chart of a major when ordered," and "failure to cease treating Belinda Mae Cerrone outside the hospital" when Springer considered her his patient. The lawyer brought in a volunteer nurse's assistant who'd thought she heard the order, but Goggin repeatedly questioned her until it was apparent she wasn't sure after all and established she was a personal friend of Colonel Springer.

Three days later, after another day of testimony, the military judge delivered the panel's verdict. Guilty.

The trial counsel came up to Goggin and Miles in the hall. "We were hampered by the definition of insubordination," Goggin said. "I think the definition should be different for medical service."

"Appeal now," trial counsel said. "You don't have much time. It's an unusual and murky case. You're right. This is medical corps. Work on it from that angle. It's Generally accepted the medical corps should be treated differently."

The appeal took two weeks. Verdict reversed. Miles went back on duty, but with the cloak of a court-martial on his record and reputation.

CHAPTER 18

Alyce Breaks a Leg

1965
Alyce

Alyce sat alone at a table for two in front of the Café de France in Châteauroux. A gentleman in a suit approached and sat in the other chair at the table without a greeting. A garçon took his order. The man took out a newspaper, refolded it with some care, so as not to interfere with those around him, and began to read. Within minutes, the sky clouded and a light rain fell, dampening the street. Alyce placed a few coins on the table, grabbed her bag, and headed for the bus stop. The military bus for the base was a few hundred yards away. She paused at the curb to let a car pass. A bicyclist came from the opposite direction, out of control, his bike vaulting over the curb, hitting Alyce from the side. She lost her balance, twisting on one leg, and fell to the ground, her leg directly impaling with all her weight on the curb. The bicycle zigzagged with the full weight of the man, toppled over and the sturdy portion of the frame landed on Alyce's leg. She screamed in pain and struggled to get up, clawing the ground, trying to reach the bus. When the driver saw no passengers waiting at the stop, he continued, unaware that Alyce was injured. She collapsed face-down on the street. The cyclist examined his bike, mounted, and pedaled off without looking down.

The man who had been sitting with her at the table, moved quickly to her side, gently turning her over. "You are well, no?" he asked in French.

She nodded reflexively, but her heart pounded. Her leg hurt, and she started to cry. The man grabbed her shoulders to steady her, and after a few minutes, he helped her stand. Searing pain made her stumble when she tried to take a step. She moaned.

"There's a doctor's office very near," he said in English. "Put your arm around my shoulder."

She hobbled forward on her good leg.

"He's a very good doctor. A friend of mine."

Even in her distress, his courtesy touched her.

The doctor controlled the bleeding from a superficial wound, gave her a pain pill, and determined she might have a fracture. She needed an X-ray and would have to go to the American base. The gentleman insisted he would take her. With the help of the doctor's nurse, they eased her into the back seat of his car.

At the base hospital, after the X-ray, she waited for the result lying on a gurney in an exam room. The man was still waiting with her until he knew the extent of her injury.

"I don't know your name," Alyce said.

"I am Antoine Villard."

She thanked him for his help in a weak, exhausted voice. "And what do you do?" she asked.

"I am an *avocat*," he said.

What kind? she wondered, dejected. She thought lawyers were mundane and hackneyed thinkers against everything and rarely in favor of anything.

"You are here with your family?" he asked.

"My father is the base commander," she said.

At the base hospital an hour later, Miles approached Alyce lying on a gurney in the hallway near X-ray. "I saw your X-ray. Fractures of the tibia and fibula that are unstable. You'll need surgery."

"I am very sorry of the result," Antoine said.

A tech prepared to push the gurney down the hall to the clinic.

"Our orthopedist is on leave," Miles said. "We'll find another hospital to do the surgery."

Antoine excused himself. "I will visit again, *Mademoiselle*. Heal well."

Alyce waited in a hospital bed with her leg elevated in traction, waiting for resolution on the transfer for surgery. The army base in Orléans had a surgeon available. Antoine Villard returned the next morning clutching a crystal vase with a bouquet of flowers that sparkled with reflected rays from the morning sun streaming through the window.

"They are beautiful," Alyce said sincerely, her voice attenuated from constant, dull leg pain.

"I am very pleased that you like them."

"Are they from nature?"

"The yellow asters and the bluebells grow wild near me. Yes. And the *pâquerettes* too. The others grow in my greenhouse."

"You grow flowers?"

"Mostly. But some herbs and tomatoes, and greens without flowers—Song of India and yucca for the house. And I care for my mother's bonsai. She is unable to care for the plants as often as she used to."

"She is not well?"

"She is hampered with pain from arthritis. But she is able to do some cooking and sew throw rugs."

"And you practice law?"

"*Avocat* is my profession. But plants are my passion."

Alyce asked about the roses in the bouquet. He touched the blooms with the tips of his fingers.

"Martagon hybrids," he said. "They have received awards."

"They are special," Alyce said. "I love roses."

"I will place them on the windowsill so you will see from the bed."

She told him of her stepmother's passion for flowers. A memory of happier times.

As he prepared to leave, he said, "Good health. And when you are better, you must come take dinner at my house. Meet my mother."

Alyce, touched by her growing value of Antoine's character, agreed. "I look forward with pleasure," she said.

"Will you have surgery?" Antoine asked as he was leaving.

"Yes," Alyce answered. "In Orléans. An orthopedic surgeon is available at the army base there."

"*Bonne chance*," he whispered to her.

***

When Colonel Springer heard the General's daughter was in hospital care, he immediately supervised Alyce's transfer to Orléans. He arranged for the newest and best military ambulance and demanded Miles take care of the paperwork. "And you go with her," Springer said, standing a few feet away from Alyce's gurney and speaking to Miles.

"But I have a full clinic schedule."

"You're the General's doctor, and you damn well will be taking personal care of his daughter's transfer to Orléans. And her return."

"I could follow after I see my patients."

"Reschedule. You ride that ambulance. Hold her goddamn hand if she needs it."

"She's not in life-threatening danger," Miles said . . . "and the ambulance crew is the best."

"Will you listen to me?" Springer leaned forward so he was a few inches from Miles's face. Springer's words were loud, and saliva frothed at the corner of his mouth. "You get your ass on that ambulance. You act like you got a princess in your care. And you be proud to serve, not your usual don't-make-a-difference-to-me shit.

"But my patients. . ."

"It's an order. You speak another word, and you'll be swallowing your teeth."

Springer turned to walk away and stopped. He glanced at Alyce on the gurney a few yards away. "This here is Ballard. He'll be with you on your visit to the specialist."

"I know him. He's my doctor. I'm the General's family," she said to Springer with muted enthusiasm. She knew Springer was well aware of who she was.

"I'm sorry, ma'am. I didn't know you were so close. But don't worry. Ballard's just for transfer. I've got you the best doc at Orléans waiting, top-notch orthopedic surgeon." Springer walked away. The ambulance driver glanced at Miles' askance with eyebrows raised, disgusted at Springer's attitude but, like Miles, compelled to tolerate it.

Miles sat on the metal side-bench that lined the wall in the back of the ambulance. He positioned next to the secured gurney that was strapped so he could monitor Alyce during the trip. It was a few minutes before they reached cruising speed on the highway.

"You didn't want to do this. Was it because of how I've acted?" she asked.

Miles shrugged. "No. Not you. I feel a responsibility to my patients."

"That Springer guy is a barbarian."

"He's weird," Miles admitted.

"Have you ever read the Gertrude Stein book I showed you?"

"I tried. But I went instead to read the history of Stein's life. I don't know how, as a Jew, she made it through the occupation alive."

"She didn't lack self-confidence."

"Did you know she went to Johns Hopkins for medical school but dropped out?"

"I doubt it was about academics," Alyce said. "I think she got bored."

"The life of the wealthy and connected. I lent the book to my friend Ingrid."

"I know her. What did she think?"

"She got tied up in the Steins's art salon and their support of new artists—Matisse, Cézanne, Braque. Picasso did a portrait of Stein. I don't think Ingrid liked it very much."

They rode in silence for a few minutes before Miles spoke again. "Why did you come to France?" he asked.

"I got phased out as a reporter at the *New York Herald Tribune*. They're in deep financial doo doo. So I talked them into freelancing, but the only place they'd let me do it was in Europe for the *International Herald Tribune*. So, with my parents here, I took the demotion rather than get fired with no job in the states and came to France."

"These are difficult times."

"Are you happy you came?"

"I think so," Miles said. "I miss the States. And many French people don't like me as an American. I was bicycling near Levroux and a motorist ran me into a ditch. I've treated two patients with minor injuries in the last couple months, cyclists deliberately forced off the road by French drivers. There's a mandate from the military police not to ride bicycles when in uniform on major thoroughfares."

I can't believe a bicyclist would do that on purpose, she thought. "Why do they dislike us?"

"It's not all of them," Miles said. "But many do resent Americans. They find us rude, bad-mannered, uncultured, materialistic. And we murder their language without trying to improve. They're intense on preserving the French language."

"But we liberated them."

"With the British and Canadians. They're not looked on with fondness either by many French."

"And there's the anti-Semitism."

"Not ubiquitous, but it's definitely here."

"And all of Europe, I guess. Besides Hitler, I've read about the Russian Nicholas the Second and anti-Semitism; even the French Vichy government arrested tens of thousands of Jews during the occupation who were transferred to Auschwitz. It's said they were told the Jews were being relocated, and they were unaware of extermination camps. That doesn't seem possible. But who knows?"

"Ingrid and Oliver are Jews and are looking for family members lost in the Holocaust, aren't they? Do they know about the French collaboration with the Vichy government?"

"Yes."

"Are they comfortable living in France? It's only been, what, eighteen years? Do they know collaborating French people arrested fellow Jewish citizens, even in the Indre, and sent them to a detention center at Drancy, north of Paris, where sixty thousand Jews were then sent to Auschwitz to be gassed? And the French-collaborators say they believed the Jews were being 'relocated to different receptive countries.' And that doesn't bother your Jewish friends?"

"I'm sure it does. It's strange. I find them special people in many ways. And they make friends like the Francophiles they are. You'll do the same. I think most of the French I've met are pro-American. Some without apathy, and many sincerely thankful for our presence—if not respectful."

"And what about you? Why did you come?"

"Drafted."

"Ouch. Sorry."

"Once I was drafted, I wanted to come to Europe. France was serendipity. And it's working out."

The ambulance braked to avoid a crash, and Alyce, held in place by restraints, slid forward a few inches on the stretcher. She said she was okay when Miles asked.

"I'm thinking of moving out of my father's place and living on the economy," Alyce said. "And I'll be traveling looking for news stories. I'll be searching for a place to live. I've started taking French. Do you know it?"

"I've got a tutor. But I started from scratch, so I'm not really good yet. My teacher is great. I could introduce you."

"I've already started courses at the base, but I'm not pleased with the quality."

Miles told of many valuable interactions he'd had with Madame Lavigne, new places he'd visited, ideas he'd discovered.

"I'd be pleased if you asked your tutor," Alyce said.

"Consider it done. I'll let you know."

The time passed rapidly; they soon arrived in Orléans.

I've misjudged him, Alyce thought about Miles. *He's more human than most doctors I've known.*

As they pulled into the ER entrance of the base hospital in Orléans, Alyce said, "I'm sorry, doctor, about that time we were flying in my father's plane to D-Day. I wasn't friendly."

Alyce reached out and took Miles's hand. "I want to be your friend," she said.

He smiled, pleased with the thought.

Miles stayed throughout her surgery and post-operatively. She was discharged in two days to remain in a short cast for six to eight weeks until the orthopedist expected she could begin weight bearing and ambulation with crutches or cane—with some pain, but not incapacitated.

CHAPTER 19

Suspicions

1965
Alyce

Two months later, Alyce's leg was better, and she was weightbearing with limited motion, but she was plagued daily with oscillating blue moods and exhausting hours of hyper excitement. She had accepted Miles's offer to introduce her to Madame Lavigne and she now went twice a week for her lessons, and she wrote drafts of articles for the paper, only one that she had submitted and was rejected.

At one of Miles's French lessons with Madame Lavigne a few months later, he asked how Alyce was progressing.

"I am very concerned, *Monsieur*. It is very personal, but I believe you should know. Now she lives with the family of Monsieur Villard."

"The attorney. I've not met him, but she has told me of his kindness to her when she broke her leg."

"I know him only from the war. We do not associate."

"Why?"

"He was an officer in the Milice. I suspect he was at least indirectly responsible for the murder of my first husband in 1944 in Tulle."

"I'm so sorry; I didn't know he was murdered."

"Yes, by the Miliciens."

"Not Germans?"

"The Miliciens were collaborators with the Vichy government controlled by the Germans. My family and most of the French patriots who fought in the Resistance fought against the Milice too."

"I don't understand. What were they?"

"It was a terrible time for French people. With the occupation, people starved. There were no jobs. And the Vichy government, French citizens who supported the Nazi leaders of the occupation, attracted support for the extermination of Jews and undesirables. French police supporting the German-controlled French Vichy government arrested French people supporting the Resistance, imprisoned them, and they sent tens of thousands of Jews to concentration camps. Most were executed. After independence, the Milice were hunted as collaborators by the loyalists. Many were tried and convicted or simply imprisoned or executed."

"And Villard was one of the Milice?"

"Yes. He was an *avocat* in Tours and his family lived on the farm near us. And he was a part of the Milice. With his silence, he condoned the murder of our civilians and Resistanance militia. We do not forgive him."

"How did he survive?"

"He escaped to South America—Argentina, I think—in late 1944. He came back in 1956. He has never been well received on his return. He has no real occupation now. He does keep hours on some days in his law office, but I think he has few clients. He sells flowers to those who do not know his past."

"Does Alyce know this?"

"I do not think so. And it is not right for me to tell her. Villard seems to treat her well. Maybe he is no longer an evil man in heart. Some think he was trapped by the cruel, immoral political movements of the time. But he is a communist and rumored to run for office. I think he will have little support. I never want him to win."

"Do you worry about Alyce?"

"He will not hurt her physically, I think. Only mental. Americans know little of the Vichy-regime collaborators and almost nothing about the Milice. They have no reason to ill-treat Villard. It's sad. Alyce is happy for the first time since her arrival. I know she takes meals with the family at times and lives in the restored house on the property."

"Yes, she is close to the family."

"She is unhappy with her parents and sister. She's adopted, you know . . ."

"I do know, and it's hard for her," Miles said. "Her father is the

General who never includes her as part of the family. All the family treat her with rejection and disrespect."

"It is probably best to say nothing," Madame Lavigne said. "Yet, if she knew his past, her judgment of Villard might not be haunted by negative secrets so often buried so close to the surface and threatening a friendship."

Miles thought for a moment. "You're right. She might resent being told, but it would be best for her to face his past and learn if it would make a difference in their relationship now."

"I agree," Madame Lavigne said. "Probably better now than later. It is inevitable, I think."

Miles had dinner with Ingrid and Oliver the same evening at their home. He discussed what he learned from Madame Lavigne about Villard. "He was nice to her when she broke her leg," Ingrid said.

"But that was strange, wasn't it?" Oliver asked. "A Frenchman, a complete stranger, helping an American, and following up like a suitor."

"She's very attractive," Ingrid said.

"And I said so to Madame Lavigne at my lesson," Miles said.

"Tall. Attractive," Oliver said.

"Not taller than Villard. And very attractive in an American way," Miles said.

"She's very natural," Ingrid said. "Beautiful in her own right."

"It does seem strange, though, that he'd be attracted to her, an American," said Miles. "And she's the General's daughter."

"What difference does that make?" Ingrid asked.

"Well, we're always being instructed not to befriend strangers. Spies are everywhere and come in different looks, and sizes," Oliver said.

"French work all over the base."

"Carefully vetted. We're in a Cold War with the Soviets. No one is above suspicion," Oliver said.

"And he's a communist," Miles said.

"And nuzzling up to the Commander's daughter could be valuable," Oliver said.

"What possibly could he learn?" Ingrid asked, who determinedly trusted everyone.

"Military strength. Types of airplanes equipped for combat. Flight destinations. Arrival of new aircraft. Wherever it's possible to insert spies into the workforce."

"Why Châteauroux?" Ingrid asked.

"We're mainly transport and have thousands of landings a month from planes from all over," Oliver said, exasperated at Ingrid's ignorance. "And he could benefit from passing base population numbers. How they're changing. How many do what jobs. How sophisticated flight support is."

"How would he find out?"

"I would think the easiest way would be to make friends with a French worker who is vetted and cleared to work on base, and he could gather any information that might be valuable. Or he could court an American close to the General."

"I don't think that's possible," Ingrid said. "Villard seems sincere. And Alyce seems loyal."

"Do you think this guy is attracted to a spinster American journalist who's not too successful at that?" Oliver said.

"I don't believe Antoine would do that," Ingrid said.

"But wooing a General's daughter, that would be a coup . . ."

"And just the possibility is enough to believe that Alyce should know . . . for her own good," Ingrid said, now suspicious even of the way Antoine had been so conveniently available when Alyce was injured in a bicycle hit-and-run.

"Is she angry enough at her family to ignore the obvious?" Oliver asked Ingrid.

"I know she feels the disregard for her from her father. I think her dislike for the General probably clouds her judgment of the motivations of all humans," Miles answered.

"That's probably true," Ingrid said.

"We should tell her," Miles said.

"I don't like her well enough to be involved," Oliver said.

Miles looked to Ingrid. "Would you do it, Ingrid?"

"I haven't connected with her well enough to be listened to recently."

"No one else has your trust," Miles said.

Ingrid shook her head in indecision.

"And it should be a woman," he added.

Ingrid nodded slowly in thoughtful agreement. It's a time in human existence when women could not trust men. That was for sure. And Alyce was a friend and Ingrid felt on that basis alone she should tell her truths about a war criminal, especially if Alyce were in love with him.

The next day at midmorning when there would be fewer customers, Ingrid asked to meet Alyce for coffee at the canteen near the main gate. They sat on the lawn at an outdoor table for two under a red-and-white striped umbrella.

After pleasantries, Alyce asked what was up.

Ingrid expressed that she, Oliver, and Miles, had discovered information that they agreed she should know about.

"Why all the secrecy?" Alyce asked.

"It's about Antoine, Alyce."

Alyce smiled. "Oh, that. I know all about that."

"What?"

"He's political. But he's not anti-American, Ingrid. He's just strongly French."

"It could be more than that. He's running for office. As a member of the Communist party."

"Everyone believes that, and he is a member of the party, but he's not seeking to run for office that I know of. And no one would run for office as a communist; less than twenty percent of the public thinks there's any value to communist leadership."

"But it's more than that, Alyce. Antoine was in the Milice."

"I'm not sure what that is," she replied hesitantly.

Ingrid believed her. Americans on the base knew few truths about the French in the WWII conflict. "Milice was a paramilitary group that rounded up Jews, undesirables, and members of the Resistance for the Vichy government for deportation," she said.

"The Vichy Government was French?"

"A government that collaborated and was supported by the Germans during the occupation."

"So it was a political group."

"The Milice is believed to have committed summary executions and assassinations."

"Antoine was never involved," Alyce said.

"Why do you think he went to Argentina?"

"He went to work there to support his family. There were no jobs during the war."

"He may have gone there to avoid prosecution for war crimes after the liberation," Ingrid said. "After liberation, many of the Milice were tried and summarily executed for their crimes. He escaped."

"That's not true, Ingrid. Antoine is French to the core. He's devout Catholic. He's a kind, generous man."

"We thought you should know. It's a history Antoine will carry with him for the rest of his life. We didn't want it to affect you."

"Why do you dislike him?"

"We don't dislike him. We don't know him."

"Why do you lie?"

"I'm not lying."

"I would never have thought it of you. You're the best Jewish person I've ever known."

"I care for you, Alyce. We all do."

Alyce gripped the edge of the table with white knuckles as she stood. "I'm living with the family now, Ingrid. Antoine's divorced sister has moved into the servant's house, and I'm living with the family. Working for Antoine at his office, too. Helping with the garden. I can't like you after this."

"Do you see your family?"

"I don't want to, and I probably never will. They have no caring for me."

"Is Antoine interested in the base operations?"

Alyce clasped her hands to hide the trembling. "He's not a spy, Ingrid. Really, I don't ever want to see you again."

"Please, Alyce . . ."

"Wash those nasty thoughts from your mind." Alyce's hands were balled into fists. Her face flushed. "You'll never have what I have, Ingrid . . . love . . . and you're jealous."

"Have you quit the paper?"

"That's none for your goddamn business, but yes. I'm submitting elsewhere."

Ingrid stood. "I'm sorry, Alyce."

"I'm so disappointed in you," Alyce said as she turned her back and walked briskly away. "And I don't want to ever read your book."

***

A month later, Alyce talked to Antoine when they were alone working in the greenhouse imbedding Lombardy poplar-tree seedlings in fortitude-soil trays to take root. She told him of her meeting with Ingrid.

"Were you in the Milice?" she asked.

He sighed, suddenly looking tired, and shook his head.

"It makes no difference to me," Alyce continued. "I don't really know exactly what the Milice was."

"I've been accused, Alyce."

"Was that why you went to Argentina?"

"It was a complicated time."

"Did you collaborate with the Germans?"

"Not in the way Americans believe."

"Not many Americans here are my friends anymore. So there's no danger," Alyce said.

Antione took both her hands and led her to a bench near the door. He turned to be able to look into her eyes as he spoke. "I knew Darnand and Laval personally in the thirties. And during the war, I did support Pétain and the Vichy government believing it was the only possible way to keep a free France. Many of us believed Germany would win, and we were determined to preserve France governed as a peaceful, socialist state. I was falsely accused of close association with Darnand because of our previous association in youth. But I was never involved in murder or assassination. I did believe that the deportation of Jews and undesirables by the Vichy regime was to support the war effort. I thought the jews were relocated. The existence of the concentration camps was hidden from most of us until liberation exposed the truth. After liberation, those thought to be associated with the Milice were arrested and many set for trial. Some were summarily executed. Revenge was rampant. I did have connections to the escape routes, and I left. It was a miserable time for me, and I returned to home as soon as I felt safe."

Alyce imagined the suffering of the Villard family and sorrow welled up inside her. Any flecks of doubt that remained about Antoine were completely displaced by empathy. She took his hand again and looked deeply into his eyes. "*Je t'aime,*" she said, her gaze lost in the depth of his affectionate stare. He embraced her. "*Ma chère,*" *he* said.

Alyce didn't think about Antoine and the Milice until she was in the *boulangerie* buying baguettes and tarts the next week. The owner exchanged the proper change as an old woman walked in, recognized Alyce, and spat angry words at her. Alyce looked back at the owner whose eyes were saturated with hatred. The old woman waited behind Alyce.

Alyce looked into the wrinkled face of the owner's brown-bland eyes, the dilated pupils. "Thank you," Alyce said.

"It is no good you live with that man," the owner said with a heavy accent of peasant French to her English.

"He is murderer of my husband. My brother saw him," the old woman almost shouted in French.

"That can't be true," Alyce replied in French.

"She tells truth," the old woman behind her said. "Many of us know how he place noose around neck of Franklin when two Nazis hoist him up to hang from lamp pole."

"Antoine Villard is a good man," Alyce said.

The woman owner took the package she had wrapped for Alyce

and handed it to the old woman. "This is now for you," she said to the old woman, who bowed her head in thanks.

"And my money?" Alyce asked.

The owner slammed coins on the counter. "Do not return."

"Why now. After more than a year?"

"Now you live with Milice."

Offended, Alyce circled past the old woman to go out the door.

The same night, Alyce told Antoine about her encounter.

"They lie," he said.

"But they both claimed to know you placed the noose around the man's neck."

"You can't believe them. It's been twenty years."

"You said you were not involved in killing the Resistance fighters. But you supported Vichy."

He took her by the shoulders and stared into her eyes. "Believe me."

"Why did you go to Argentina?"

He let go of her. "To avoid arrest as a collaborator. I am not a killer."

Alyce lay alone that night in her bed. He did not come to her. She passed the hours wondering where the truth hid. Doubt had invaded her, and she wondered if she would ever consider his proposals of marriage again.

At her next lesson, Alyce confronted Madame Lavigne about the photos. Madame left for an upstairs room and returned with a stack of five folders. She opened the third and showed a photo of a man hanging from a lamp pole, and two men not in uniform standing at the foot of the ladder propped against the pole. A few feet away was an officer with a military cap that shadowed part of his face.

Madame pointed to the image. "That is him in the uniform of the Milice, is it not?"

"His face is dark. It's not Antoine," Alyce said.

"Many have identified him from this photograph."

"I don't believe it."

Madame slipped two other photos from a folder. "This is at a parade in Vichy. Both show Villard standing in uniform reviewing the troops."

Alyce had no doubt now. "This is not killing. Everyone knows he was Milice but he denies murder. And this is not evidence!"

"It is hard to prove murder after the happening," Madame admitted.

Alyce left Madam before the lesson was over and drove directly to Antoine. "I'm so sorry," she gushed. "I should have never doubted. Please forgive me." After a long pause where Antoine seemed to iron out his thoughts and feelings, he kissed Alyce on both cheeks. They were reunited.

PART FOUR
1965

CHAPTER 20
Toussaints

1965
Miles

On a Wednesday in April 1965, Miles went for his twice-a-week French lesson with Madame Lavigne at the *Boulangerie*. She sat at a table with two chairs in an upstairs storage room surrounded by shelves with metal molds, baking pans, bowls, dishes, lidded jars—some with labels—sacks of flour and tins of sugar stacked in a corner where a window looked out onto the street. "Sit," she said in French, bypassing her usual pleasant greeting and without looking up. "Today we will discuss General De Gaulle's *La Discorde chez l'ennemi*." She looked up with a tenuous smile, her face flushed, her eyes wet with tears.

Miles remained standing, anxious to know what was bothering her. He'd never seen her like this. "What's wrong, Madame?" he asked.

"It's really nothing. Please sit. We will start," she said.

"Is there anything I can do?"

She paused for many seconds.

"Please, Madame," he said.

She sighed. "It is *maladie* in the family, *Monsieur*. The daughter of my cousin is extremely ill. I worry there is nothing to do."

"How old is she?"

"She has eleven years."

"Is she in hospital?"

"She is at home."

"Does she have a fever?"

"She is very hot to touch. How do you say—groggy? And she coughs much."

"Has it just come on?"

"Oh, no. More than a week."

"Does she have a doctor?"

"Oh, yes. He is doctor of family for many years."

"Is she getting better?"

"This morning my cousin called and said she is hard to wake up. I have dread."

"How is she being treated?"

"She take medicine."

"Do you know what?"

"The usual for cough and fever."

"I'm worried, Madame. Please call to find out what she's taking?"

Madame hesitated, but again looked at Miles earnestly with his silent pleading to help.

"I will call. The phone is downstairs."

They went downstairs and she called her cousin Monsieur Toussaint, the father of the sick girl. She spoke urgently in French, too fast for Miles to follow.

"She is given bryonia and antimuonium tartaricum," she said to Miles.

"May I talk to him?"

Monsieur Toussaint spoke English well. Miles confirmed the treatment, asked about symptoms, past history, and allergies. He placed his hand over the phone mouthpiece.

"She is very sick, Madame. If I could examine her. Suggest treatment. Please tell him I am not licensed in France, only the United States, but that I'm fully trained at the best American hospitals."

Madame discussed Miles's proposal with her cousin. The conversation turned animated for a few seconds, then calmed. "He was not sure, but I convinced him," Madame said. "He said to come as soon as you are available."

"We should go now," Miles said.

"They live near Tours."

"We should hurry then."

Miles drove to the hospital to get medicines before departing. The majority of French people believed and relied on homeopathy, even so, Miles was sure the girl might be treated with remedies that probably had little or no effect for a serious condition.

In an hour and thirty-five minutes, they were at the Toussaint home. Madame Lavigne's cousins were an upper-class family who lived in Athée-sur-Cher, near Tours, in a modest château near the Cher River. Period French eighteenth-and nineteenth-century antiques furnished the home. Miles paused at the size of an antique, four-poster, canopy bed that diminished the slender girl-patient named Clémentine. The Toussaint family—father and mother, Clémentine's older sisters, Manon and Sophie, and a housekeeper—gathered around, silent with concern as Miles made his evaluation.

Droplets of perspiration speckled Clémentine's forehead, a luster-less sheen dimmed the details of her brown eyes. Miles asked Madame Toussaint to help hold Clémentine in a sitting position as he listened with his stethoscope to Clémentine's chest; the breath sounds in the lower lobe of the right lung were absent, replaced by crackles and wheezes. Her productive cough sounded dry and scratchy. She had a viral pneumonia with secondary bacterial infection, and there was no doubt her medicines had worsened her condition.

Madame Lavigne translated as Miles spoke in English to the family. He emphasized the severity and the danger of her pneumonia. He added the urgency to stop Clémentine's medicines. Monsieur Toussaint looked to each member of his family for their approval and, after a pause, he agreed but with noticeable doubt of the correctness of his decision. Madame Lavigne quickly thanked Miles. The family remained silent, clearly anxious about the wisdom of the change in treatment.

Clémentine's temperature decreased within three hours. She smiled for the first time. Miles said he would return the day after next to examine and gave instructions for reaching him if needed before then. There were no objections.

Madame Lavigne stayed with the family and Miles drove back to Châteauroux, thankful that Clémentine was improving. For five days in the evenings after work, he drove the hour and forty-five minutes each way to the Toussaint's to monitor Clémentine's progress.

***

After a week, as Miles checked her, Clémentine smiled at him. Her older sisters, Manon and Sophie, and Madame Lavigne were again at the bedside.

"She is better, doctor. No?" Manon asked.

Clémentine's temperature was normal, and her breathing had improved. Her right lung was still slightly congested but breath sounds were sharper.

"You fly airplane?" Clémentine asked in French.

"My cousin told her you were in the American *armée de l'air*," her mother said.

"You fly, yes?" Clémentine persisted to Miles.

"Clémentine . . . " her mother cautioned.

Miles smiled to indicate he didn't mind Clémentine's questions. "I do fly in very big airplanes," he said in the best French he could muster, "but best of all, I'm learning to fly a small private plane by myself."

"Oh, will you take me for ride, *Monsieur, s'il vous plaît?*"

"I would love to—when you are completely well, and when I'm all trained and have my license. We'll do it!"

Clémentine coughed before she smiled with pleasure.

Sophie requested instructions for care. After explaining, Miles gave her medicines, and gave another injection of antibiotic to Clémentine.

"You speak English with such perfection," he said to Sophie, "I only hope I can do as well in French someday."

"Already you speak very well," Sophie said.

"Madame Lavigne is a very good teacher, but I must have more practice to gain confidence."

"Well, she is known for her skills. And you can practice with me and the family."

"How did you learn English?"

"We are taught in school. And I spent four years in England at Oxford."

"What was your major?"

"I studied art history. I hope to teach at university."

"Here?"

"It is possible. But I want to learn first to create my own art."

Miles said he admired her career.

As Miles arranged his medical bag, Sophie thanked him for his treatment. Madame Lavigne, relieved at Clémentine's progress, asked if she could return to Châteauroux with Miles.

"Of course," he said.

Madame Lavigne remained rigid with her hands clasped as they began the drive back to Châteauroux. Miles drove with extra caution, and she seemed to relax.

"Thank you for what you did for Clémentine," she said.

"She's special."

"You saved her life. We all believe that."

"I was worried about her medicines, not only that they may not have value, but they may have been ineffectual and prevented necessary treatments."

"The doctor is a longtime friend of family. He was upset in the beginning. But he became supportive. He admitted the value of having you."

They rode in silence for a while.

"Thank you, Madame," Miles said. "You have a wonderful family."

"They like you," she said.

They were lost in their own thoughts for the remainder of the trip. As Madame left the car at her house she paused. "I know they will invite you to Nice for the holidays. Mardi Gras. They have a house there that is in the family. I hope you'll be able to go."

"I'll be sure to make time to get away," Miles said.

CHAPTER 21
Talents

1965
Miles

Three weeks later, Miles returned with Madame Lavigne to the Toussaint Châteaux to complete a follow-up examination. Manon met them as they emerged from the car.

"*Docteur* Ballard," Manon said, "come with me to the library. Clémentine has a surprise for you."

Miles and Madame followed Manon to the library. There were two chairs positioned for them near a grand piano. The family and the housekeeper gathered around behind them as they took their seats. Clémentine entered and with measured grace mounted a small rectangular platform near the piano a few yards in front of guests and family.

She wore a short-sleeved white dress trimmed in lace with a red sash at her waist and patent-leather red Mary Janes with ruffled, turn-cuff white socks. Her golden hair had been combed and held back with a white ribbon. Still, errant hair strands drifted down to cover her face, which she swept back at intervals. Smiling politely, she began with a nod-of-the-head bow directly to the audience, then recited:

> "*Le Renard et Le Corbeau,*" by Jean de La Fontaine.
> "The Fox and the Crow," she said in English.

Miles did not know the story, but with Clémentine's animated and polished French delivery, he was able to follow the gist.

> *Master Crow perched on the highest branch of a small tree and held a piece of cheese in his beak that he had stolen from the ledge of an open kitchen window.*

The wise and crafty Master Fox loved cheese and was attracted by the smell. He quickly devised a plan.

"Well, hello Mister Crow!" the fox said. "How pretty you are! You seem beautiful to me!"

The crow preened with pride.

Clémentine frowned with displeasure.

"I do not lie," continued the fox, 'if your voice is like your plumage, you are the phoenix of all the inhabitants of these woods."

With these words, Clémentine tapped her temples with pointed index fingers to emphasize the clever intelligence of the fox.

Crow is overjoyed. To show off his beautiful voice, he opens his beak wide . . .

Clémentine held her arms out, palms together and pulled them apart, one up and the other down, like the crow opening his beak to sing.

"Caw caw croak caw," the crow cackled . . . and the cheese fell to the ground."

Clémentine lowered her gaze to her feet, where the cheese would have been.

"The fox grabs it, and says: 'My good friend, you must learn that every flatterer lives at the expense of those who listen to him."

Clémentine raised her hand with her index finger pointing up and spoke slowly and distinctly with gravity.

"The crow, ashamed and embarrassed, cried out in despair.'"

> "'Do not lose heart. My lesson,' said the fox, 'is without doubt, worth the value of a piece of cheese.'"

Clémentine put her palms to her temples and shook her head in disbelief.

> "The crow, mortified, swore he would never be fooled again by a flatterer."

As family and guests applauded, Madame Lavigne whispered to Miles, "It is a fable every French school child memorizes."

"She did very well."

Madame Lavigne nodded.

Clémentine turned and went to sit on the piano bench to open the keyboard-cover.

"Tchaikovsky's theme from *Swan Lake*," Madame Lavigne whispered to Miles.

Clémentine proceeded to play with control and relaxed patience for four minutes with only two instants of hesitancy. She stood and bowed, beaming with pleasure at the end.

As the audience stood, Miles went to Clémentine. "Great," he said.

After the performance, Miles examined Clémentine. Her lungs were clear, her temperature normal, and he declared her healthy. He then took the blood pressures of all those in the room and made notes to keep in his bag to compare if he ever saw them again.

Sophie led Madame and Miles to the drawing room, where she served *gaufres à la flamande* with coffee.

Madame Lavigne stayed at the Châteaux to spend more time with her cousins, and Miles began the drive back to Châteauroux alone. He felt calm and pleased to have witnessed the caring of the family for Clémentine and their delight in her performances.

CHAPTER 22
Paris

1965

Miles and Ingrid worked at their easels facing each other as Bruce worked at a slight distance away at his permanent workstation. It was their Thursday evening painting session. On a canvas, thirty-six by forty-eight inches, Ingrid had blocked, with the edge of a palette knife, outlines of horizon, sky, and buildings in the town of Loches, on the Indre River between Châteauroux and Tours. Then she used a sable brush with a pale wash to suggest details of Saint Antoine tower in front of the Château de Loches, farther in the background.

"I like what you're doing," Ingrid said to Miles as she worked.

"I'm finally following Bruce's directive when we first started, trying to get the sunflower yellows right contrasted to foliage greens and sky blues in that field on the way to Déols," Miles said. "I'm having trouble with my sky."

"Here, try a transparent Prussian blue." Bruce tossed Miles a tube of paint.

Miles mixed the Prussian blue with titanium white. He held the palette so Ingrid could see. "What do you think?"

"Might work well," Ingrid said. "You might mix a touch of Indian yellow, too, and less white."

"Good thought," Bruce said.

They all worked in silence for a few minutes.

"What's Oliver doing this evening?" Bruce asked.

Ingrid laid her brush and palette on a stool and wiped her hands on a cloth rag. She closed her eyes with her head down, reluctant to try to respond. "He's been busy," she finally said. "At work. He bought that part ownership in the Bumpy Landing as an investment. It takes up a lot of his time." She dabbed a wetness at the corner of her eye with a clean corner of her paint rag so no one would notice.

"Do you have any trips planned?" Bruce asked Ingrid.

Ingrid stared at the floor, her body tense. "Not at the moment."

I shouldn't have brought it up, Bruce thought. *Her marriage must not be going well.*

"I do have tours on the new arrivals for the military. But no personal plans," Ingrid continued.

"Let's do a visit to Paris for art," Miles said. "Invite your friends."

"It wouldn't feel right without Ollie," Ingrid said.

"Of course, ask Ollie," Miles said. "Would you and Ina be available?" he asked Bruce.

"It would be great."

"We'll book rooms near the Louvre," Miles said. "And I can ask Madame Lavigne if she would like to go. She has family in Paris and knows the art community well."

"I know Madame Lavigne works in restitution of art stolen by the Nazis," Bruce said. "She's amazing."

"She's intense," Ina said.

"She'd be perfect," Ingrid said. "I know little about the recovery of the stolen art."

"It will give us all an uplift from the blues," Miles said.

***

Madame Lavign arrived two days before and stayed with her artist niece, Manon Toussaint, who owned a commercial art gallery. Ingrid, Miles, Bruce, and Ina arrived Friday afternoon. Oliver had declined the trip.

Early on Friday morning, Madame Lavigne rang a bell at a side door of the Jeu de Paume, the museum of art on the north corner of the Tuileries, which was closed to visitors at that time of day. A museum staff-member greeted them. They all entered.

Inside, Mademoiselle Rose Valland, the director, emerged from an office, shutting the door behind her. She was petite with short dark hair and round, horn-rimmed glasses on a plain face without blemishes, and a persistent look of concern and anxiety. *She looks in her sixties,* Ingrid thought without malice. She wore a pale beige summer dress patterned with small flowers and a large white collar and a three-inch black leather belt fastened at the waist.

"Mademoiselle Valland, I'm Manon Toussaint . . ."

"No,no, no, no, no. I know you. We've met, what, four times? And, of course, I know your father."

"This is my cousin, Margaux Lavigne, and her student in French, Ingrid Stern, who lives in Châteauroux at the airbase," Manon said. "And this is *Docteur* Ballard, who has treated our family."

Rose Valland remained silent for a few seconds and Ingrid worried she had an attitude toward the base and the Americans. But then Mademoiselle greeted her and kissed her on both cheeks. As Mademoiselle Valland embraced Madame Lavigne, she said, "I still grieve the loss of your husband at Tulle."

"Thank you. I've recently saw a photo of him hanged from a lamp post in Tulle in an American magazine," Madame Lavigne said. "It brought back so many upsetting memories."

"What a disgrace," Mademoiselle Valland said.

"And the perpetrators at the Nuremberg trials only scratched the surface of the guilty," Madame Lavigne said.

Mademoiselle Valland showed the guests where paintings damaged by the thefts were being restored. There was another open space where other works of art were being authenticated and researched for the history of their ownership before German occupation of France. Then Mademoiselle Valland invited them to a ceremony at the Louvre.

Extensive press coverage and art aficionados packed the Louvre ceremony with a crowd of more than three hundred. The Minister of French Culture led a ceremony displaying three recently recovered paintings, confiscated by the Nazis in late 1942-43, to be returned to their rightful owners. Mademoiselle Valland was honored and the Minister presented a history of her work in recovery, and in her life-threatening work as a spy when the Germans stored tens of thousands of historically and artistically valuable paintings and works of art in the Jeu de Paume. She was praised for her continued work with the Monument Men. The Minister listed her awards as the most decorated woman in France.

That night, the Châteauroux group went to the opera and had a late dinner with Manon. After dinner, Manon asked Ingrid if she would like to stay in Paris for a while in her apartment at her *galerie d'art*. Ingrid excitedly agreed.

The Châteauroux group left the next morning.

Ingrid spent more than a week staying in an apartment above Manon's gallery. She learned about the operations of probably the most successful gallery in Paris at the time. As Ingrid prepared to leave, she asked if she could learn by filling in managing sales and inquiries when needed.

"Of course," Manon said. "I'd like that. I hoped you might have interest."

"And when I come to Paris," Ingrid said, "I'd like to be more involved in the recovery of stolen art."

"I'll personally arrange a meeting for us with Rose Valland. I know the Ministry of Culture wants to involve Americans. Many paintings have been recovered in the United States. Recovery is an exhausting and time-consuming task. They'll be thankful for your interest. And I'll call you when I visit home next month in the Indre," Manon continued. "I'd like you to know my family."

Ingrid was proud and grateful and said so.

CHAPTER 23
Mardi Gras

Nice
1965

After the Christmas holidays, Miles received a formal invitation from the Toussaints to stay at Madame Toussaint's brother's home with the family in Nice for Mardi Gras. Miles took leave-time for a week, and on the Thursday before Mardi Gras, with Madame Lavigne, he drove eight hours to a villa—a legacy from previous generations—owned by Madame Toussaint's brother-in-law, Crowder Emhoff. The Emhoffs were not there; they spent February, March, and April vacationing in the Antilles, where they rented a house in Willemstad on the island of Curaçao and, on many days, sailed their sixty-meter yacht among the islands. The Emhoff art-deco style, two-story villa was built in the early 1920s and stood on a hill in the Mont-Boron area. Painted a pale yellow and with off-white columns in front on both levels, it provided expansive views of the city—the 11th century castle, the promenade, and the Mediterranean Sea.

In private, Madame Lavigne made it perfectly clear to Miles that the Toussaints were respected and of modest means compared to the excesses of the brother-in-law, who was indolent and extravagant, she implied. To Miles, they all lived so far above his lifestyle he felt uneasy in their presence for reasons he did not fully comprehend.

***

The next day, Monsieur Toussaint had business with a financial advisor in Monaco. Madame Lavigne stayed at the villa with Miles and Madame Toussaint while Clémentine, Manon, and Sophie went first to see their grandmother, who lived near the promenade, before they turned to shopping in the city for materials and costumes for Mardi Gras. Clémentine chose a hooped-skirt dress of green and purple, a white peephole mask, and a sunburst headdress. She picked out a brass scepter burnished to a glistening sheen.

At the villa, Madame Toussaint served breakfast for Miles and Madame Lavigne of pastries, confiture, fresh fruits, and coffee—on the terrace in front of the villa. The view through clear air was over the wakening town to where the Mediterranean Sea dovetailed on the horizon with a resonant, turquoise sky.

"Madame tells me you were active in the Resistance," Miles said to Madame Toussaint.

"That was twenty years ago," Madame Toussaint said. "I was twenty-five years old. Margaux was the heroine." Madame Lavigne flushed at the compliment. "The Germans killed her first husband in Tulle."

"It was Sophie Toussaint who carried messages about German activity to resistance leaders," Madame Lavigne said. "She was only twelve and constantly in grave danger."

During the day, they watched parades on the Promenade des Anglais with dancing women, flowers, cultural and historical themes, and floats with tableau vivant and giant figures of political and cultural celebrities. Teams of trim women in sparse costumes marched and waved flags and banners, wearing garlands and holding bouquets of fresh flowers. Acrobats on six-foot stilts circled the floats. Colossal helium-filled balloons bumped along the route, tethered with ropes held and heaved by individual crew members. Marching and walking participants interacted with the crowds, greeting, and throwing bundles of stemmed blossoms.

In the evening, they went to city central where high rows of stadium-style seating were situated in the square facing a large open path for the parades. The Toussaints had coveted seats three-quarters of the way up in the stands. The parade started as the sky darkened to night. Soon, flares, Roman candles, starbursts, serpentines, and crackers ignited the dark sky, obliterating the stars. Eighteen floats carried gigantic papier-mâché figures, often articulated, of characters exquisite or grotesque, all brightly illuminated with endless colors of purple, stark gold, forest green on vermillion, crimson, mauve, black on russet, blood-red on cornflower blue. Bands played, majorettes strutted, costumed riders on horseback wove among revelers as crew members on the floats threw trinkets and beads from elevated positions. Cannons propelled confetti skyward into the human sounds of merrymaking, frolic, and dance that pulsated through the air.

The Tousiants with Miles sat in a row of plank-seating high up in the stands. Clémentine sat on a seat next to the aisle, then Monsieur Toussaint, Madame Toussaint, Manon, Sophie, and Miles.

The crowd noise intensified as a float featuring Joan of Arc on horseback at the Battle of Orléans came into view. Clémentine, using her father's shoulder for support, stood on the plank seating as two men descended the steps in the aisle next to her. The younger man tripped and fell into an older, heavyset man who lost his balance falling forward knocking Clémentine off the seat. Clémentine plummeted down the stairs in the air headfirst, hitting a stair, and somersaulting into the seats only to have her momentum thrust her back into the aisles where she continued to fall to the base of the stairs where she lay, crumpled and silent.

Miles was instantly on the move down the row taking the steps two at a time. Amidst the crowd noise in the stadium, the individuals near the accident were frozen still and silent, unsure of what to do.

Miles reached Clémentine before anyone could recover from their shock and kneeled at Clémentine's side. She was breathing in gasps without signs of pain. Miles cradled her head between his hands and gently moved it into a straight position with the spine. Her look to him showed more surprise than fear.

He spoke to her, raising his voice to be heard above the crowd: "Breathe deeply and try not to move. Stay calm."

A stranger reached out to straighten her twisted torso.

"Don't touch her," Miles spoke abruptly. Then he said to Manon, who was now kneeling next to him, "Keep them away. Send for an ambulance."

Manon called to her father to contact emergency. Dazed, he

hurried off to find police authority. An attendant appeared. Miles instructed him to disperse the crowd and all but immediate family as far away as possible. Sophie reached for Clémentine's hand, but Miles told her firmly not to touch her, his tone implying it might cause further damage if the spine was injured. He touched the skin on Clémentine's legs, but there was no reaction, no movement. The twisted position of her body indicated spinal injury. He had to keep the body motionless until help arrived with equipment to stabilize her.

Now Clémentine's moist eyes looked vacantly into the continuously ebullient festival sky. She said nothing, her lips trembling.

Thirty minutes later, an emergency crew arrived with the combined expertise and equipment to raise Clémentine onto a gurney for transport. The ambulance departed, and the Toussaint family gathered to find transportation to the hospital. Miles joined them.

***

Three days later, after surgery, the family and Miles were informed of Clémentine's paraplegia. It was partial and it would be months, maybe years, of intense rehabilitation before the degree of improvement could be determined.

CHAPTER 24

Lessons

1965

In November, on a visit to Clémentine for a health care checkup, Miles learned Clémentine's tutor in Tours had died, and the Toussaints had not found a replacement. At dinner with Oliver and Ingrid, Miles mentioned Clémentine's sadness, and Ingrid suggested Agnes Colletti.

"Perfect, if she'll agree to do it," Miles said.

Ingrid went to Agnes's house in Brassioux the next morning. "We are very fond of the daughter of the Toussaints, whose passion is playing piano. She is very talented. Her piano teacher has died, and she is without an expert tutor. Would you consider teaching her?" Ingrid asked.

"I don't like children," Agnes replied. "Best thing I ever missed was childbirth and responsibility for a young one."

"Clémentine is not a child, Agnes. She's thirteen now and from a distinguished family. She is educated and very intelligent."

"It's not what I want to do, Ingrid."

"But she's depressed without activity to improve something she really loves. Think of it as therapy for a child with paraplegia who deserves the best. And as a favor to me. I would greatly appreciate it."

"It's too long a drive. Major Bonnard doesn't like to drive in France."

"Either Miles or I could take you. We both want the best for this girl. Would you like a glass of wine? I've brought a bottle of Chassagne-Montrachet for you."

"I've never taken to a hard sell, Ingrid."

"Please, Agnes. It would be a good deed."

"I've never been a humanitarian."

"She's a human being that needs you. You are the best."

Agnes shook her head with incredulity at Ingrid's persistence-of-persuasion.

"You'll never regret it," Ingrid said.

Agnes frowned for a few seconds and looked to Ingrid with a perplexed smile of concession. "I'll try," she said, "but only a trial!"

Ingrid leaned forward and kissed Agnes on both cheeks.

Miles took Agnes on her first visit to teach Clémentine. Grumpy Agnes had little to say.

"You don't seem excited about this," Miles said to her in the passenger's front seat.

"I let Ingrid weasel me into it."

"You could have backed out."

"Not with Ingrid."

"This is gracious of you, Agnes. Clémentine is capable and deserving of the best."

"Pooh."

"You're the best."

"Ingrid has already said that. You don't have to swizzle me."

"I'm not a swizzler," Miles said.

"Knowing yourself is the beginning of wisdom."

"Aristotle, isn't it?"

"No mind. It's the truth."

The lesson was in the music room of the château, Clémentine had a special stool that lifted her higher than normal and a footstool that supported the braces on her legs. She was dressed in a light blue cashmere sweater and a brown wool skirt. She sat on the piano bench, her wheelchair behind her. Agnes stood next to her to be able to see the keyboard and the music on the intricately carved walnut music-rack.

"Good," was all that Agnes could allow as praise for Clémentine although she knew her playing was exceptional.

"You love birds?" Agnes asked Clémentine.

Clémentine nodded.

"You know the oriole? His song?"

"I do." Clémentine thought for a few seconds. "Do, da, do, da," she went from high to low. And then up—"do, dee."

"Yes. Many oriole breeds use those intervals. Thirds and a fifth, I think." Agnes reached out and closed the music folder on the rack. Now, I don't want you to think about what the notes look like. You remember what the oriole sounds like. Play what you remember."

Clémentine played what she sang.

"Do you see the notes on a staff?"

"If I think about it."

"You have close to perfect relative pitch. I want you to hear and then play. Nothing visual. Ready?"

Agnes sang a series of eight notes. Without hesitation, Clémentine played the notes in pitch exactly as Agnes had sounded.

Agnes repeated other notes in a lower key. Clémentine responded. Then in a higher key. Clémentine responded again without any hesitation.

"Did you visualize *those* notes on a staff?" Agnes asked.

Clémentine shook her head. "Not really."

"Good. We're going to continue next time, after our classical piece, to work on playing by ear. Not by memory of notes on a staff, but creating from imagination. It's an example which many of the classic composers must have learned when writing music inspired by nature. Birds chirping, changing seasons, volatile weather. Listen to Vivaldi's *Four Seasons*."

"Where can I find the recording?" Clémentine asked.

"I would think the music store in Tours."

"Do you play jazz?"

"I'm learning."

"How do you do that?

"There is a staff sergeant on base who leads his own combo. He lets me practice with them. Blues, mostly. I learn the harmonies, improvise on the melodies, accent the rhythms."

"Can I do that? Sophie loves jazz."

"We could work on it after classical instruction. It would cost more. Would you like that?"

"Oh, yes," Clémentine said.

"We'll include that in the next lesson. Do you have jazz LPs?"

"Sophie does. She goes to nightclubs in Paris."

"Listen to some of them and tell me what you like best."

"Well done," Miles said to Agnes on the way home. "I've played blues harp for years. Mostly to records. Would you introduce me to the sarge?"

"I believe that's not allowed for commissioned officers, is it? He's Negro," Agnes said with an unusual touch of hesitancy in her voice.

"We'd be making music," Miles said, "not fraternizing."

Within three weeks, the Jazzman Jenkins Quartette became the Jazzman Jenkins Quintet, with Captain Miles Ballard on blues harp. There were no complaints about race.

***

In September, Ingrid walked to Miles's quarters. "Did you know Agnes is going to marry her major friend . . . the bird watcher?

"Really?"

"A surprise, isn't it? Who would have thought of Agnes marrying?"

"I can't imagine Agnes as a romantic, either."

Ingrid smiled. "Maybe helping Clémentine made her a better human being."

"Closer to likable, maybe," Miles said.

Ingrid handed him a folded piece of notepaper without an envelope. "An invitation she wanted me to give you as soon as possible."

Inside the fold of paper in a too-tightly-gripped-pen handwriting, Agnes invited him to her wedding ceremony.

CHAPTER 25

Surprise

1965
Agnes

On a late Saturday afternoon, Ingrid went with the Toussaints to Agnes Colletti's wedding to Major Bonnard. Miles went straight from work to the pre-ceremony reception. Fifty-seven invitees attended.

A raised platform and white-painted folding chairs were arranged on the tendered lawn of the farm of a friend of the Major's. Minutes after Ingrid's arrival, Agnes, breathing determinedly, took Ingrid firmly by the arm and led her to the edge of the crowd where they couldn't be heard.

"I'm calling off the wedding," Agnes said.

Ingrid couldn't think of a response.

Agnes carried on. "I'm going to announce it before the ceremony."

"Does Major Bonnard know?"

"Not yet."

"He's got to know," Ingrid said. "You can't just surprise him at the altar."

"I haven't told anyone."

"Why are you doing this? Is it just being in France? The isolation? Not knowing the language?"

Agnes was lost to tell her feelings. *He doesn't talk to me when we're alone,* she thought. "He's getting old," she said.

"Everyone is."

"Not like him. He doesn't have the energy to make new friends. His memory is going; he vegetates; his emotions are flatline. I'm ashamed of how I feel, but it never ceases to irritate me."

"He's depressed?" Ingrid asked, feeling the source of Agnes's actions.

"I would be his caretaker, not his companion. What would you do?"

Ingrid thought for a few seconds, sympathetic with Agnes's dilemma. "Do what you feel is right, Agnes. What are you planning?"

"A new life in Paris. I now have friends in the music community, and I'm going to teach piano and organ. I'll play in a cathedral, and I've been asked to play and teach daily in the workshop of an internationally famous organ maker."

"Is this your real reason for backing out?"

"I was planning to take him with me to Paris. But I don't think I could stand it."

"Then you must tell him now, Agnes. Before your announcement."

"Couldn't I just leave?"

"That's not right."

"I could leave a note."

"Look. Dismiss the priest. Tell the quartet to play for two hours more. Then take the Major with you to the platform, and gather the audience, and tell them!"

Agnes paused. "I'm losing my nerve."

"You can't wait." Ingrid said. "And you're the one to do it. Believe that you're doing the right thing for both of you."

Agnes trudged off.

Agnes found the Major coming out of a porta-potty. She blurted out her decision, avoiding explanations that tumbled inexpressibly in her mind.

The Major shrugged.

"Is that all you can say?" Agnes said with a flare of anger.

"I've been expecting it," he said.

"Really?"

"We're not alike, Agnes. It would be a mistake to marry," he said without passion.

"Glad to have that straightened out. Let's get this over with, then." She turned to start toward the platform.

But the Major stopped her and took her hand. "Relax," he said. "Look composed."

He led her calmly to the podium with a microphone. He squeezed her hand when she tried to let go.

Agnes took a deep breath to begin her confession. "Thank you for coming," she said timidly, but the Major interrupted and addressed the crowd with the force-of-command of a general.

"Attention please," he said. "Gather round. We have an important announcement to make." Without urgency the crowd began to move, and the Major repeated his announcement two more times so all would hear. Even with the crowd gathered, he still had not released Agnes's sweaty palm. He thanked all for coming this afternoon, thanked them for their friendship. He hoped their understanding would keep friendships as sustainable as they have always been. "We have an announcement," he said, pausing and gazing over the crowd. "We've decided not to marry."

A silence ensued. Agnes was thankful that she heard no gasps, then worried why there had been none.

"Agnes and I are the best of friends and always will be," the Major said, "and we wish the best to all of you—our friends. We love you all. Please enjoy the music and the party. Stay for as long as you want."

After faint applause, Agnes spoke, her voice high and strained. "The bar is open until the last person leaves," she said. "When you do leave, please take food with you, we'd feel terrible if it wasn't enjoyed. Bye!" She waved like a child going off to summer camp.

The Major helped Agnes down from the platform, dropped her hand, and they separated.

Agnes went to Ingrid. "How did it go?"

"Fine," Ingrid said.

"I didn't expect him to speak, but he did well, don't you think?"

"You both did well." Ingrid thought Agnes's exhilaration was poorly timed.

"Could we have our usual lunch tomorrow at the restaurant?" Agnes asked.

"Of course."

"That's great." Agnes turned to a group of friends to face questions she did not have answers for.

CHAPTER 26
Bob Goggin and the General

1965

The General took Bob Goggin to Scotland as his lawyer, ostensibly for official consultations about air strength and US support for the United Kingdom if attacked. The meeting was in London, but the General and high-ranking officers had reservations at the Old Course at Saint Andrews after the meeting. The General played golf poorly, and usually surrounded himself with quality players to detract from his inadequacies.

On the return trip, Goggin saw an empty seat next to the General, vacated by his aide who'd gone to the bathroom. Goggin rushed forward and sat down.

"What's up, Goggin?"

"Well, sir, I wondered if you were aware of what happened to Captain Ballard."

"Of course. He was my private physician, for Christ's sake. And you guys were friends. I'm sorry he left the service."

"Yes, sir. And I was also his lawyer at his court-martial for insubordination that ignored the lives he saved and the thousands he healed."

The aide came back down the aisle toward the General. The General raised his hand and pointed a finger at an empty seat a few rows away.

"So what do you want?" the General asked.

"Miles wasn't treated well by the Air Force, sir."

"He was acquitted."

"Yes, sir. After an appeal, but he was harassed by a few officers who thought him guilty of insubordination. Officers who are best friends of the colonel who brought the charges."

The General knew all the circumstances of the court martial, and

Goggin was well aware that the General didn't like Springer personally or professionally.

"Miles was the best GMO we've had, sir." Goggin stared at the General with unwavering conviction. He continued, "He was loved by patients. He devised programs. He persisted in follow-up. He formed a research project on suicide."

"Get on with it, Goggin."

"Well, sir, Miles found a surgical residency program at Charity Hospital in New Orléans not up to his satisfaction. He has applied to schools of public health. He wants to work broadly in the delivery and support of healthcare in General. Because of his service in France, he never had opportunity to develop contacts in the field who might write him the outstanding letters of recommendation he deserves."

"And that's what you want, a recommendation?"

"He treated you."

"He's kept me alive."

"Treated your daughter."

"Never push it with my family. That's personal."

"Would you write him a letter of support based on his integrity, skills, work ethic, personality while medically serving the Air Force in France?"

"You can't be asking me that. I treat all personnel the same. And I don't write letters of recommendation to medical schools."

"Yes, sir. I understand. But I've got a list of the schools and appropriate individuals. Addresses. Bios. Just in case you might have the opportunity." Goggin pulled out a folded piece of typing paper with his handwriting and eased it into the General's hand.

"Goggin, you're beyond belief. Did Ballard put you up to this?"

"Absolutely not, sir. You know he's not like that."

"But you are, aren't you? Well, the answer is no and never mention this conversation to anyone for your own sake." The General frowned as he worked hard to absently tuck Goggin's folded paper into his inside coat pocket.

"Thank you, sir."

"Be warned. I'll do nothing with this. It's not my place. It's inappropriate."

"Yes, sir." Goggin stood to retake his previous seat and the aide quickly repositioned himself beside the General as Goggin walked down the aisle. He'd gotten further than he ever imagined with the General, and he was pleased to believe the General would help if he could.

PART FIVE
1966

CHAPTER 27
Destiny

1966
Boston

Ingrid now worked full time at Manon Toussaint's gallery, titled *D'Art D'Art* as in Paris, on Newbury Street in Boston. She lived in a third-floor apartment in the gallery, had her office, as manager, on the first floor, and oversaw seven staff. Early on a Monday morning, before customers became numerous, Ingrid sat at her desk she had rearranged to where she could watch the front door to personally greet customers. Emily Lodge entered timidly opening the door. Ingrid hid her face with her hand and went to a cabinet under the stairs to the second level to appear busy. She never wanted to see Emily again. Too late. Emily rushed forward and cornered her.

"Ingrid. Ingrid Stern! You look wonderful."

Ingrid felt a sharp pain in her chest at seeing Emily and searched for words. She avoided a greeting; her memories of Emily in France didn't allow a warm reception. "May I help you?" she asked. "I'm the manager. Mrs. Batten, isn't it?"

"I've never used that name, Ingrid. Lodge will do. And please call me Emily again."

"May I show you the gallery?"

"I love *D'Art D'Art*. A favorite gallery."

At first, as they began a tour, Ingrid instinctively avoided any hint of camaraderie. She showed Emily around the gallery for more than an hour with aloof formality until she was convinced of a different Emily than she remembered.

"You seem to know the collection," Ingrid said as they stood near the exit door.

"I come to the gallery every few months. It is one of the galleries on my list to visit as a board member."

"I've never seen you?"

"You've changed your desk. You saw me when I came in."

Ingrid softened. "I'm glad you did, Emily. I enjoyed the visit."

"I've always worried about meeting again. The memories of my action in France. I was so unwell."

Ingrid waited for Emily to continue.

"I was clinically depressed, Ingrid. I remembered what you had said about my life. I went into therapy. Hospitalized for two months with sessions twice a week after I was released. I still take Librium."

"Are you divorced?"

"Parker? Oh, yes. My analyst said my marriage was a major contributor to my illness. Oh, my," Emily grabbed her shoulder bag. "I've got to go. Doctor's appointment. Could we have dinner together tonight?"

"I'd like that," Ingrid said sincerely.

That evening they dined together at Durgin-Park.

"And now I'm estranged from Mother, who has refused to be civil to me since the divorce and tried to prevent me from marrying Lionel," Emily said. "I still feel occasional guilt about disliking my mother. But without her, I have more confidence; I've made a circle of friends, my own friends. And Lionel is perfect for me. A professor at Boston University College of Fine Arts. Not rich, middle class, and that drove mother to distraction. 'You can't marry beneath you,' she yelled, which made me all the more eager to begin life in my own way."

"I'm so glad you're better, Emily," Ingrid said.

"What about you? Have you remarried?"

"I didn't realize how unhappy I'd been until I wasn't married anymore," Ingrid said. "My ex-husband was court-martialed for dealing drugs, spent a year in prison, was dismissed without honor from the service. He practices somewhere in Idaho now."

"What happened to all your friends from France?"

"We have a round-robin letter that we circulate for everyone to add to throughout the year."

"Your husband was a doctor at the base, wasn't he?"

"He was of my mother's shadchan selection. And we did well for four years. But he was so openly unfaithful, it became demeaning."

"Have you found someone else?"

"Mother found a prospect for me, again with a Jewish shadchan. But he's much older than I. Shy. Insecure. Educated but dull. And I've given up on him, and don't see him anymore. And Mother and I don't speak to each other."

They talked over dinner for more than three hours.

As they were leaving, Emily said, "I forgot to ask. Do you do acquisitions for the gallery, too?"

"Sixty percent. Mostly American. Some Canadian, but the Canadian quality isn't as desirable for us. The owner, Manon, has the most valuable contacts in Europe and she ships stock every three to four weeks. We're doing a good business."

"You're well respected for your eye and quality."

"Thanks. Manon has been a friend and a teacher. I learned buying and management from her in Paris."

"When I see what you've done, would you permit me to place your name for a position on the acquisitions committee at the Museum of Fine Arts?"

"Am I qualified?"

"More than qualified with your studies and experience. And the board would be especially interested in your work with restoring Nazi art-thefts to their original owners."

"I met Mademoiselle Valland many times in Paris. And Manon and I helped recover two paintings and a sculpture from Germany and a painting from Italy."

"May I propose you as a committee member?"

"Please do," Ingrid answered, warm with pleasure.

***

Emily and Ingrid became friends; Emily accompanied Ingrid on a buying trip to Montreal, they worked together at the MFA, they attended concerts and lectures. Ingrid wrote to Miles, now still in New Orleans, out of the military, and intent on finding a new career other than surgery for himself.

Dear Miles,

You can't imagine how much Emily has changed. It's remarkable. She is now estranged from her mother, and finally, her mother is out of her life as recommended by her analyst. She does see her father once a week. I've met him twice and genuinely like him. Her new husband is a little wonky at times about political opinions and never misses a Red Sox game—even away games— but Emily doesn't seem to mind. They love each other, and I'm happy for her.

Excited that you're playing blues harp with street bands in New Orleans. Would love to hear you play. I write to Agnes often. She made the right decision to not marry. She is giving lessons on piano and organ in Paris, and with her near perfect relative-pitch and skills, is paid by restorers to help tune organs, especially the older ones. She has many friends and speaks French very well now. She has no contact with the base but visits the Toussaints twice a month to help Clémentine with her progress.

Emily has plans for a trip to Paris with a few friends for two weeks. She and Lionel are paying for airfare and lodging. I know she will ask you, and I hope you'll be able to go.

Miles was still working at Charity Hospital but gave notice as he awaited responses from Public Health residency programs. He was anxious about his chances.

He received a handwritten invitation from Emily and Lionel within days. He called to thank her personally, and apprehensive about her motives when she met him for the last time in Châteauroux, to sense her new disposition. She had changed. He wasn't sure who she really was now, but there was no doubt she was a different person.

After a few hesitant moments on the phone from both, he doubted any awkwardness would come from Emily. She assured him that he would be on his own with time in Paris to visit friends from his time in service.

In late May, Miles flew to Boston Logan to transfer to the transatlantic flight to Paris that Emily and Lionel had arranged. He saw Ingrid for the first time in more than two years when boarding the flight. His ever-present affection for her swelled inside him and he greeted her with great warmth and camaraderie.

At the hotel, all the travelers were making arrangements for dinner. Ingrid asked Miles if he were free. He smiled widely with a boost of vitality.

"Where do you want to go?"

She suggested *Le Grand Véfour* that had three Michelin stars, served exquisite food, and was within walking distance of the hotel.

They were seated facing each other at a table for two next to a mirrored wall that reflected views from windows to the exterior.

"It's been way too long," Ingrid said. "I'm so glad to see you," she repeated for the second time since they'd met.

"You haven't changed in the least," Miles said.

"What did you expect?"

"My memories. We had wonderful times together. Art at Bruce and Ina's. The trips. Thank God for your letters."

"And you yours."

"How are things at the gallery?"

"It's special working for Manon. I'm in charge now, and she spends much of her time with her family in Athée."

"Sophie wrote me that Clémentine is mobile now with braces and crutches," Miles said.

"I spent a weekend every month with the family until I left,"

Ingrid said. "Manon is doing bronze sculpture in Paris. She's made me a part owner in Boston. We have a staff of twelve now."

"Twelve?"

"That includes restorers, framers, appraisers, marketing, sales. And we have more than fifty contributing artists and requests to show from hundreds of others."

"Pleased for you. Do you go to New York often to see family?"

"My family ignores me, Miles. I haven't been an ideal daughter—divorced, barren—blamed for a hysterectomy before I was twenty to remove a tumor threatening exsanguination. Mother looks everywhere for someone suitable. She found a widowed Jew at synagogue, in his sixties, desperate for a wife after his second wife died. He was short, bearded, misogynist, and mostly non communicative. I refused. Mother never forgave me. What about you? What's happening?"

"It's strange. The residency in New Orleans was all operating—sixteen-plus hours on, eight or less off, for weeks at a time. No academics and no research. But I love the city. Food, music, atmosphere, art, hard-working people. When I could get a break, I'd second-line in a funeral parade just to share the joy of people taking their dead comrade to the next world. They truly believe Jesus will welcome them into the hereafter—where the blues don't get you, you get weekends off, and people really seem to love each other."

"Are you leaving because of surgery?"

"I do want something different. I think it's being a doctor who is always on call, treating one person after another. It's mechanical—an assembly line of human suffering. You just put them back together anatomically and physiologically as best you can with what you have. You think of all the souls that you never have chances to heal. And you never have enough help or resources to do your best."

"What is it Emily's mother said about you?"

"'His time and his brain are taken up with working on his Humpty Dumpties,' or something like that. I really want to work with health care systems and deliver quality health care equally for everyone. And I want time for myself, develop as a human being who cares rather than a mechanic who repairs."

"We did help people in France, didn't we?"

Miles nodded. "And the military. But it's France that I miss. Do you?"

"Oh, yes. Vibrant times in an artistic culture. We were so fortunate. Would you go back?"

"I don't have the finances now. But I will go back. I dream about it."

"I miss the French way of life'" Ingrid said, "and the people who live it."

"Madame Lavigne, the Toussaints . . ."

"And Clémentine is an elegant young lady now. She thanks you."

"I'd like to see her and the family. The friends from Châteauroux."

"And Alyce?

"Oh, yes. I haven't heard details about her relationship with Antoine for a while. In fact, I'm renting a car and leaving tomorrow to visit friends in Châteauroux."

"Really, I was going to take the train."

"Go with me. It would be great having you."

"Wonderful!" Ingrid smiled, her brain filled with exciting images of her next few days with Miles.

***

They stayed three nights with the Toussaints. They took Clémetine to a festival at the Château de Chambord. Clémentine used a wheelchair for the visit but spent most of her regular days ambulatory with crutches.

On the second night, they had dinner with Alyce. Antoine wasn't available.

Alyce had completed her book on the war and submitted it to a publisher. Ingrid said she was still working on her book on the Holocaust. Alyce seemed withdrawn. Miles glanced at Ingrid to let her know he felt about Alyce and Antoine.

"Is everything okay between you and Antoine?" Ingrid asked gently.

"Oh, yes. Of course. Although his mother died. I rarely see him because of his political ambitions in Paris. I'm busy writing for the American press, and I live mostly with Father and Mother. My sister ran off with a staff sergeant. Antoine's family doesn't really like me."

"What is the effect of the US military leaving France?" Miles asked.

"Almost no presence now. The General is being transferred to Vietnam next month. Mother will go back to the States."

"Are you going to stay here?"

Alyce paused, her eyes dampened with emotion. "I don't know. Antoine is waiting till after the election. He knows he won't win and plans to spend more time on the farm."

"And you like the farm life?"

"It's not that. Antoine is impenetrable most of the time. He loves me in his way. He knows no other way. His life has been without serious emotions of love. I'm beginning to think I need something more. Maybe I'll go back to the States with Mother."

"Was he changed by the war, Alyce? Being with the Milice, escaping to South America?" Miles asked.

"I've begun to doubt his denial of involvement again. I think he still anguishes over his involvement in the war. He rejects charges of violence, but I think he's unwilling to remember the past. We have an opaque curtain between us to keep us from confronting things we both have buried."

"More wine?" Miles asked Alyce.

"Please," Alyce said.

Miles signaled the waiter.

Alyce said Madame Lavigne and her husband had sold the *Boulangerie* and had retired to southeastern Spain. Miles wrote down the address as he and Ingrid departed after dinner the next night.

"I don't want trip this to end," Miles said. He led Ingrid to a wrought-iron seat for two away from the path overlooking the Cher River. "Can you arrange more time off before the flight back?"

"How long?"

"Ten days. Maybe two weeks?"

"Leave on the twenty-eighth?"

"We could make it a travel vacation. Portugal? The French Alps."

She took his hand and put her head on his shoulder. "I have hoped for something like this." She kissed him on the cheek.

***

They spent two days in Aix en Provence. Miles, out of courtesy and respect, booked separate rooms for each of them. On the second night, Miles heard the connecting door open to his unlocked room in the haze of his light sleep. The bed shimmered as Ingrid sat on the down quilt.

"Miles," she said.

"Hmm." He felt her breathing, the scent of her absorbing him. The cover unfolded back as softly as a cloud slipping over a mountain range, and she was beside him. Without speech, he held her—his heart kneading his chest—with a gentle firmness as to never let her go. They made love slowly, every touch a pleasure, every whisper a rapture, their dreams united, their souls as one.

They had breakfast in the room in silence the next morning, smiling and gazing at each other. They drank coffee on a sofa holding hands.

"A walk?" Ingrid asked.

He kissed her on the lips. They dressed and walked a five-mile trail through the forest to a plunge waterfall splashing into a deep punchbowl pond. They couldn't let go of each other. Dehydrated from the exercise, they lifted water from the pond to their mouths with cupped hands, the water leaking through the cracks among fingers. They carried on still in silence, communicating a love they both had longed for. They returned to the hotel hungry and happy. They ate an early supper in the restaurant and went to bed in his room together. He held her. "I love you," he said. She cried happy tears and undressed for bed.

The next morning as they packed to leave for the States, Ingrid said fretfully, "What are we going to do, Miles? I don't want to go on living without you. It's been too long already."

He stopped packing. "We've got to figure something out. I'll have to change my plans for school—"

"No, no. You can't do that. I'd feel guilty and you'd always wonder what could have been and would it have been better. I could ask Manon about opening a branch gallery of *D'Art D'Art* where you settle."

"I can't let you do that."

She teared and crossed the room to hold him. "We can work out something. Have faith."

"I will. I promise," he said.

***

They returned to Boston on the same flight. Arrival was midmorning, and while Miles waited for his connection to New Orleans, Ingrid sat with him. They enjoyed the special awareness of being together again, a blessing, but avoided talking about how they might erase the physical gap between them until the plane was ready to board.

"What can we do?" Ingrid asked. "Maybe I could ask Manon to find me work in New Orleans."

"Maybe I could find a teaching position in Boston. I could do academics. I'm anxious about my chances."

"But anything is possible. You have so much to give."

But not probable, he thought.

"We can find a way."

He gazed into her eyes. *We need to commit to our future.* "Don't you think it's time we got married?"

A cry of joy escaped her, loud enough that passengers turned their heads. They embraced as if to bury themselves forever in a clasp of mutual caring they had avoided for so long."

***

In New Orleans, Miles took a taxi directly to the hospital to work a night shift for a friend. The next morning, he returned to his second-floor apartment in the French Quarter. His landlady heard him squeezing his bag through the door and brought him two weeks of unopened mail she'd collected to prevent theft while he was gone. An armful.

Scattered among bills and advertisements, letters from universities were easily spotted by the official envelopes. He tore open the glued flaps one by one. UCLA, Johns Hopkins, and Maryland had turned him down; Tulane, Columbia, and Harvard had accepted him. He called Ingrid long distance.

"I'm coming to Boston."

"When? Can I pick you up at the airport?"

"Not today. I mean I'm *moving* to Boston."

"I don't understand."

"Harvard accepted me. I'll be in school in Boston."

Ingrid cried with joy.

Short Stories by William H. Coles

*The Activist, The Amish Girl, The Bear, Big Gene,
Captain Withers's Wife, The Cart Boy, Clouds, Crossing Over,
Curse of a Lonely Heart, Dilemma, Dr. Greiner's Day in Court,
Facing Grace with Gloria, Father Ryan,
Gatemouth Willie Brown on Guitar, The Gift, The Golden Flute,
Grief, Homunculus, The Indelible Myth, Inside the Matryoshka,
Lost Papers, The Miracle of Madame Villard, The Necklace,
Nemesis, On the Road to Yazoo City, The Perennial Student,
Reddog, Sister Carrie, Speaking of the Dead, The Stonecutter,
Suchin's Escape, The Thirteen Nudes of Ernest Goings,
The War of the Flies, The Wreck of the Amtrak's Silver Service*

Books by William H. Coles

*Guardian of Deceit
The Surgeon's Wife
The Spirit of Want
Sister Carrie
McDowell
Facing Grace with Gloria and Other Stories
The Necklace and Other Stories
Story in Literary Fiction: A Manual for Writers
Literary Fiction as an Art Form: A Text for Writers
The Short Fiction of William H. Coles 2001-2011
The Illustrated Fiction of William H. Coles 2000-2012
Creating Literary Stories: A Fiction Writer's Guide
The Short Fiction of William H. Coles: 2000-2016
The Illustrated Short Fiction of William H. Coles: 2000-2016
The Art of Creating Story*

On Amazon Kindle
WILLIAM H. COLES Literary Fiction Story

www.ingramcontent.com/pod-product-compliance
Lightning Source LLC
Chambersburg PA
CBHW060919250626
47159CB00008B/3082